JULIA JARMAN

A TEST FOR THE TIME-TRAVELLING CAT

ILLUSTRATED BY DAVID ATACK

Collins

An imprint of HarperCollinsPublishers

For Tom Brocklehurst

First published in Great Britain by Andersen Press in 1997
First Published in Lions by Collins in 1999
This edition published in 1999
Collins is an imprint of HarperCollins*Publishers* Ltd
77-85 Fulham Palace Road, Hammersmith, London, W6 8JB

1 3 5 7 9 8 6 4 2

Text copyright © Julia Jarman 1997
Illustrations copyright © David Atack 1997

The author asserts the moral right to
be identified as the author of the work.

Printed and bound in Great Britain by
Caledonian International Book Manufacturing Ltd,
Glasgow G64

ISBN 0 00 675298 5

Chapter 1

Topher Hope turned the key in the door of 35 Arburton Road. It stuck a bit at first and he thought it wasn't going to open. The lock was a modern one – with several burglar-proof devices in it – though the door was old-fashioned like the house. Peering through the coloured glass Topher could see Ka sitting on the black and white tiles of the hall floor, haloed in the afternoon sunlight.

She was staring at the door – and he longed to feel her fur beneath his hand. He loved this time of day, the hour or so they had together before his dad came home from work. He thought about it from time to time while he was still at school.

'I won't be a sec, Ka.' He jiggled the key in the lock, thrilled that she was there. Because she wasn't always, though she usually appeared quite soon, from the top of the house, or from the back garden through the cat-flap in the kitchen door.

The front door opened at last.

'Mwow!' She was beside him in an instant, winding herself round his legs. He stooped to stroke her, and she jumped on his back, then onto the hallstand, then onto his shoulder. He watched her in the hallstand mirror, rubbing her head against the side of his. She was the most beautiful cat he had ever seen – he'd never stop thinking that. Her golden fur flecked with black and white rippled as she purred ecstatically.

Topher . . . rrr. Topher . . . rrr.

She seemed to speak, sometimes did speak.

I'm so pleased to see you.

The ankh – the key-like mark on her forehead, which was the Egyptian sign of life – shone, glossy and black, as she gently head-butted him. Her amber eyes were huge, the pupils mere flecks in the sunlight.

'Don't ever leave me, Ka.' He spoke to her reflection. She had left him once. It had been dreadful, till he'd found her.

Never . . . rrr. Never . . . rrr.

He could feel her purrs as he stroked her throat.

'If you go, you must tell me.'

Of cou . . . rrrse. Of cou . . . rrrse.

She sprang down and set off towards the kitchen, her too-long tail stuck in the air. He followed. 'And you must take me with you.'

But now she was more interested in food. One leap and she was on the draining board nudging her dish towards him. He reached for some Whiskas and the tin opener.

'Out of the way, Ka.' For an intelligent cat, a remarkably intelligent cat, she was a bit stupid where food was concerned. 'You'll get your whiskers caught.'

She was pushing his hand with her head, but he managed to open the tin without trapping any of her long white whiskers, and as she ate, nosing the bits she didn't like over the edge onto the floor – like any fussy cat, except for her exceptional beauty – he thought about how extraordinary she was. She had travelled to Ancient Egypt once, and so had he!

Sometimes, looking at her and looking at himself, he could hardly believe it had happened. Nobody would call him exceptionally anything, though his friend Ellie's mum said she envied him his blond hair.

Ka finished eating, then said, 'Mwow,' in a particular way which meant *Sit down, Topher, I need your lap*. So he went into the sitting room, picked up the TV guide and settled himself on the sofa. Then he turned to Tuesday's programmes, and Ka appeared beneath the guide, making it impossible to read. *Put it down, Topher. Put it down. Pay attention to me.* So he picked up the remote control and flicked through the channels. There was tennis – Wimbledon was on – a lot of children screaming in a game called Finders Keepers, or Plucky Duck. He watched the cartoon – with difficulty – as Ka settled herself right under his chin.

The news was on when he heard his dad's key in the lock. 6.15, it must be. His dad was a creature of habit. No. Only five past. Unusual. You could usually set your watch by his dad's movements. He heard his voice and another voice, a woman's, saying his dad's name. Topher

7

and his dad were both named Christopher Hope, so one was called Chris and the other Topher to avoid confusion. It had been his mum's idea.

They came into the room, his dad and the woman. She was tall, like his dad, but with smooth black hair – his dad was a bit bald. Her hair was like his mum's, he couldn't help thinking.

'This is Topher, Molly. Molly, Topher.'

Her name didn't suit her. Mollys were soft and jolly with rosy cheeks. Farmers' wives. This one was pale and she wore glasses, sunglasses – so he couldn't see her eyes.

She stuck out a hand. 'Hello, Topher.' And she took off her glasses. 'What a beautiful cat.' She had grey eyes.

'I told Molly I made a mean Bolognese sauce, and she's come home to sample it.'

Mean? His dad trying to be trendy. It was embarrassing. Molly was younger than him. That must be why.

'I'll go and get started.'

Molly followed his dad out of the room and Topher heard her asking his dad if he'd mentioned her to him.

Ka woke up and stretched.

'I don't like her, Ka. I don't like her.' He said it quietly, hardly said it at all really. It wouldn't have been so bad if it had been Sylvia, the freckly one. He'd got used to her, and she was good on computers. His dad said he had to have friends because he'd been lonely since Tessa had died. Tessa was Topher's mum. She'd died in an air crash, two and a half years ago. It still hurt to think about that. Ka purred and rubbed her cheek against his. *Don't wo . . . rrry. Don't wo . . . rrry.*

8

Later, when he was in his bedroom doing his homework, revising for a tables test, his dad came in.

'What's the matter, son?'

'Nothing.'

Molly had gone it seemed. Dr Molly Carstairs had gone. She was a doctor, his dad said, not the medical kind, though she worked in medical research. She was a scientist.

'Molly's trying to find a cure for cancer,' he'd said at dinner trying to make conversation. He thought Topher would be as impressed as he was. But Topher wasn't.

'I expect she experiments on animals,' he said later to Ka.

Chris Hope said, 'Sorry. I should have told you I was bringing someone home, but it was a spur of the moment thing.' He sat down on the bed.

Topher didn't say anything.

'We agreed we'd talk about things, Topher. Not bottle things up, you know.'

That was true. They'd agreed, because at first after his mum died, they hadn't talked at all. They'd both been scared to admit how bad they felt. But what was there to say now?

'You didn't like Sylvia at first.' His dad wouldn't give up. Surprisingly, that was true too.

'Ka liked her, Molly I mean.'

So was that true. Ka had jumped on her knee while they were at the table, and Molly had let her lick her plate.

'And she liked Ka.'

'You'd have told me off if I'd let Ka lick my plate.'

'Molly *had* finished eating.'

9

Even so, Ka had sat on her knee while she drank coffee too.

When his dad had gone Topher turned to Ka who was sleeping on his pillow.

'Traitor.'

She opened one eye.

'Move over.' Topher climbed onto the bed and Ka climbed onto his knee. She started to purr.

You could be wrrr . . . ong, Topher.

'Shut up.'

Be fai . . . rrr. Be fai . . . rrr.

Eventually he told Ellie about his dad's new girlfriend – because that's what she was – it was obvious. They went out with each other several times and they saw each other every day. Molly lived in a flat round the corner. They both travelled to work on the Northern line.

Ellie Wentworth was Topher's best friend. They were both in the top class at St Saviour's and Ellie lived quite near, with her noisy family in Cheverton Road. She was a bit deaf. She'd been very deaf till she'd had an operation which gave her back most of her hearing. You still had to speak very clearly to her. Topher told her on the way home from school. She'd asked him what the matter was because he was so quiet – even for him – and he said his dad had a new girlfriend who was cruel to animals, and Ellie was really shocked. She thought she'd been cruel to Ka.

'What did she do?'

Topher had to explain, that she – Dr Carstairs that is – experimented on animals.

'How do you know?' Ellie, with her head on one side, looked like an alert dog.

Topher said, 'You must have heard about what they do. There's been loads in the papers.' Once someone had given him a leaflet about it.

Ellie said, 'What sort of research?'

'Medical. Cancer. My dad thinks it's wonderful.'

He thinks she's wonderful was what he thought.

And Ellie said, 'Couldn't that be all right? I mean, I expect they practised my operation on some animals before they did it to me.' She laughed. 'My dad says he hoped they did. We've talked about this a lot.'

The Wentworths talked about everything. They never stopped, and now they were at their house. All the windows were open and he could hear Russell and Luke, her younger brothers, arguing. There was pop music coming out of the windows too. It was a wonder the neighbours weren't complaining. The houses in the street were all joined together in a long terrace, the same as Arburton Road. You had to be very careful about noise.

'That's another thing,' said Ellie, as Muggins her black and white kitten appeared on the wall. 'Animals.' She stroked Muggins between the ears. 'If scientists didn't test drugs on animals, they wouldn't have any drugs to cure animals with when they got ill, would they?'

He didn't answer and she went on. 'Muggins had his injections yesterday, so he won't get enteritis or cat leukaemia. They're both fatal diseases. He'd die if he got them.'

Topher said he was going home.

That night his dad was quieter than usual – and so was

Topher. It was awful, just like after his mum had died – and his dad burnt the pork chops. Topher said it didn't matter, he was thinking of becoming a vegetarian anyway.

His dad said, 'I don't think Ka would like that.'

Fortunately she seemed to like the burnt bits.

That was all they said. After dinner his dad wandered from room to room aimlessly. There was something the matter. Topher didn't ask what. He went upstairs to play on the computer in his bedroom. Later, as he lay in bed he heard his dad pacing the floor downstairs.

In the morning, as he went out of the door to go to work, Chris Hope said, 'I'm sure you'll be pleased to know that Molly has got a new job. She'll be moving away from here. Soon.'

When Molly – or Dr Carstairs as Topher preferred to call her – came round next, it was a fortnight later on a Friday. She had presents for everyone, even Ka. Ka's was a sprig of catmint. Dr Carstairs held the grey-green leaves under her nose – there were some small blue flowers too – and Ka went barmy. She grabbed the mint and rolled over and over with it, holding it against her nose. It was the smell she liked, but the smell wasn't enough for her, she tore at the leaves with her little front teeth and ate them. Then she lay stretched out on

12

the kitchen floor, with a smile on her face.

Even Topher laughed. It was as if Ka was drunk on the minty smell.

Dr Carstairs said, 'I wanted to see if she liked it. Some cats go crazy for it, others couldn't care less. I've got lots in my garden. I'll bring you a root of it before I leave.'

She brought Topher a book called *The British Museum Book of Cats*. It was one he'd wanted for a long time. There were some marvellous photographs in it. There was a picture of Bastet, the Egyptian cat-goddess, on the cover. He had seen this statue, when he'd visited the museum, and he'd found out a lot about Ka. Ka was an Egyptian word meaning a double. That's why he'd given her that name. She was the double of a carving his mum had given him. She was exactly like the carving – but only Topher knew why. He'd explained to Ellie once, but wasn't sure if even she believed him. Suddenly his dad said, 'Have you shown Molly your Egyptian cat, Topher?' He turned to Dr Carstairs. 'Tessa gave him a little statue of an Egyptian cat just before she died.'

Topher felt himself reddening. He couldn't show Dr Carstairs the statue, and he didn't want to, and he still felt uncomfortable when his dad mentioned his mum to other people.

'Topher?'

'No.' Sometimes his dad went too far.

Ka followed him upstairs. The statue wasn't on his bedside table where it sometimes was *because Ka was*. It was the statue *or* Ka – how could he explain that? Today Ka was a living cat. Here. Now. On the floor looking up at him. He stood in front of the sash window, looking over the rooftops of a London hazy with heat. The unusually good summer weather had lasted for weeks and there was an almost permanent smell of barbecue in the air. People had moved outside to their gardens or roof terraces. Mrs Ewing on their left was in her garden snuffling around near the fence, probably spying on his dad and Dr Carstairs who were on the patio two floors below, their heads close together. Topher closed the window.

She, Dr Carstairs, came round one more time, to say goodbye she said, and to bring the promised catmint, a big clump of it, which she divided into three and planted in the back garden, after much consultation with his dad as to where they should put it. Eventually they put one bit beside the shed at the bottom of the garden, one in the border beside the path and one in an old sink beside the back door. She found the sink behind the shed. He helped her carry it up to the house. Then he fetched a can of water and poured it wherever she told him to.

'Try and keep Ka off it till it's rooted,' she said to Topher. She'd made a little cradle of twigs round each plant to help keep her off. 'And water it well in this weather. Once it's established you'll probably find her sleeping in it, but if she uses each patch in turn they'll probably survive.'

Then she went – very quickly – saying she didn't like prolonged goodbye scenes and just when Topher thought that one problem at least was solved, Ka disappeared.

Chapter 2

She wasn't at the end of his bed when he woke up the next morning – it was a Saturday – and she didn't appear during the morning. But he didn't worry terribly at first. Ka was a free spirit like all cats. She couldn't be kept in a cage like a rabbit, or just taken for a walk like a dog. She chose where and when. And her double, the stone replica of herself that stayed behind when she went time-travelling, wasn't beside his bed. So maybe she had just gone wandering in the neighbourhood, by the old railway line perhaps. Almost certainly she was all right.

Unfortunately Ellie found the carving again, when she came round later that morning. She was looking for something to read, and suddenly there it was, in her hand, the little statue of Ka. She'd found it behind some books.

She said, 'You should look after this better, Topher.'

He took it from her without saying anything. So she hadn't believed him; she hadn't understood. The statue was cold, almost like ice, though furry with dust. In the bathroom, he rinsed it under the tap, and the colours sparkled, Ka's colours – gold, black and white. But when he dried it on a towel and placed it beside his bed it looked dull and lifeless again.

Ellie said, 'We could go for a walk and look for Ka.'

15

He said, 'There's no point.'

She was time-travelling, there was no other explanation. He'd just have to wait till she came back.

'Topher Hope-less!' Exasperated, Ellie got up. Why hadn't she understood when he'd explained? She went downstairs. A few moments later he heard her calling out of the back door. Then he heard the front door slam.

Where was Ka?

When was Ka?

He picked up the book Dr Carstairs had given him. Chapter 1 was about the ancestors of the domestic cat. There was *felis* this and *felis* that but he couldn't concentrate on that stuff. So he flicked through looking at the pictures instead. There were Egyptian cats and Japanese ones, Roman and Greek ones. There was a photo of a cat's pawprint in a Roman tile in Silchester. The Romans

almost certainly brought cats to England – and rats. There weren't any of them here before the Romans came.

So where had Ka gone this time? Back to Ancient Egypt or somewhere else?

There was quite a lot about Dick Whittington and his cat, which was an unusual story for its time. In the fourteenth century it was risky to own a cat, specially a black one, in case someone said you were a witch. And the Tudors in the sixteenth century – they were doing the Tudors and Stuarts at school – weren't any better. They thought witches could turn themselves into cats! A man called Topsell wrote: '*It is most certain that the breath and savor of cats consume the radical humour and destroy the lungs, and they who keep their cats with them in their beds, have the air corrupted and fall into hectics and consumptions.*' Stupid man – some people were allergic to them, like now, it was obvious. But some people must have liked them enough to let them sleep in their beds, but most had a terrible time. 'Throughout the sixteenth and seventeenth centuries cats were subjected to appalling torments . . .' No, he wasn't in the mood for reading! He put the book down, and a few minutes later Ellie returned – his dad must have let her in. She said she hadn't seen Ka, but she had seen Lisa Carney who had seen her last night, at about half past eleven. She'd been outside number 58 making their dog bark.

'When did you last see her, Topher?'

He tried to remember. She'd been on his bed when he fell asleep around ten.

That night when he went to bed, he made sure that the

17

carving was on the table beside his bed where he could see it. He lay on his side observing it carefully. Sometimes, when it was about to come to life in the middle of the night, *to become Ka*, it glowed. It didn't glow that night. As he lay between sleep and wakefulness he tried to banish from his mind the more gruesome images he'd seen in the cat book. Dr Carstairs should never have given him it.

'I hope you're not in Tudor times, Ka. It wasn't a good time for cats.'

It was a miserable weekend. His father, a serious person at the best of times, looked glum. He spent most of Sunday in his study, but when Topher glanced in he didn't seem to be doing much work. His computer was switched on, but he spent most of the time just staring at the screen. Computers were his thing; he taught computer science at the university. Topher guessed that he was missing Dr Carstairs. It made him feel a bit guilty for being glad she'd gone. Topher missed Ka. In a few days' time the school holidays would begin. He'd be lonely without her. His father had made extensive arrangements for what he called 'care' during the six-week break, though Topher had told him he didn't need to. He didn't mind being on his own some of the time, as long as he had Ka. The house seemed cold and drained of colour without her.

His father blu-tacked a timetable of holiday arrangements to the kitchen wall. Some of them weren't too bad. He was going on an art course during the first week. He'd asked to do that. He wanted to try his hand at pottery. He would really have liked to do sculpture, but there weren't any courses on that. He sometimes thought

18

about the person who had made Ka. Did he – or she –
know what a wondrous creature he had made?

On Sunday night he went to bed quite early before it
was dark, but it was shadowy in his room at the top of
the house. It was an irregular shape with lots of corners
and the ceiling came down at odd angles, and when he
switched on his bedside lamp, the stone cat immediately
looked more life-like. A gust of wind lifted the curtains
and her large translucent ears seemed to flicker. Seemed
to – he watched for a long time – and he wished there
was something he could say, some incantation he could
utter which would breathe life into the stone.

'Come back to me, Ka. Come back. Come back.'
Nothing. It was a good job no one could hear him.
They'd think he was mad.

'Cric-crac. Come back.
Cric-crac. Ka.
Cric-crac. Come back. Come back from afar.'
Nothing.

Then over the rooftops and through the window came
a peal of bells from some church or other, and he tried
another tack.

'Turn again. Turn again. Turn again, Ka.
Loveliest cat of London.
Return to me.'
It didn't work and he fell asleep.

But when he woke up in the middle of the night it
was happening!

Chapter 3

He'd seen it happen only once before. Then, it was as if something was breathing life into the stone, was gradually turning stone to fur. This time, it was as if something in the stone was trying to break out. The gold shone, seemed to smoulder like molten metal; it seemed to be burning, growing brighter and brighter as he, suddenly upright, watched, mesmerised, too scared to breathe. White flecks sparked and the black lines were like cracks in the stone's surface. Was the statue simply cracking up?

'Ka?'

There was no answer, but the table beneath the cat vibrated. Then claws sprang from the stone, flexed like tiny cutlasses.

'Mwa!' The mouth opened revealing pink flesh and sharp white teeth.

'Mwa-a! T-touch me, Topher!'

He put out his hand, then hesitated. The surface still looked burning hot.

'Touch me!' she gasped, and he stroked her head, between her flattened ears and felt velvety fur beneath his fingers!

'Ka!' Joyfully, he moved his hand down her back which arched beneath his touch. He could feel the bones of her spine.

Then she sprang. In one leap she was on his bed, beneath the covers, her fur against his bare skin.

He could feel her trembling against his stomach.

'You're all right now, Ka.' He lifted the duvet slightly, and her large eyes shone out of the darkness. That was all he could see. The pupils were round like moons.

'Mwa!' It was a cry of distress.

He wanted to hear her purr. 'You're safe now. You're with me.'

It was obvious she had been in danger. Stroking her, he felt her bones beneath his hand. She was thinner than when she'd left, much thinner. Her skin was taut and her fur seemed stiff and spiky.

'You're okay. You're okay.' He tried to soothe her with words and the warmth of his body, for she was cold to the touch. He'd been wrong about the heat.

'Why are you so cold, Ka?'

'Mwa!' She wasn't telling.

What had happened to terrify her like that? 'Where have you been, Ka?'

She didn't answer, but slowly – oh so slowly – she calmed down and he felt her muscles slacken. She began to lick herself clean and the fur beneath his fingers grew warm and silky soft.

'You must never go back there, Ka. Wherever it was. Promise.'

He waited for her purr. *I·prr . . . omise. I prrr . . . omise*. But it didn't come. She didn't purr. But eventually she slept, and so did he.

In the morning she was still there against his stomach. It was as if she hadn't moved all night – and now, lifting the duvet, he could see her.

'Good morning, Ka. Welcome home.'

The sun shone in, spotlighting her. She made a soft chirruping noise in her throat, pleased to see him. But when he ran his hand through her fur she flinched.

'What is it, Ka?'

She backed off at his touch, and seemed to cower beneath the covers.

'Are you hurt, Ka? I've got to look.'

She wouldn't let him, so he went downstairs for her breakfast, brought it upstairs and placed the dish on his bedroom floor. Then as she ate he knelt down and managed to examine her. There was an angry red mark round her neck, where the fur had been rubbed off, leaving raw skin, broken in places. It was as if someone had tried to strangle her! He remembered one of the pictures he'd seen – of exactly that – and tried to banish it from his mind. But then he noticed the book open beside his bed. 'Throughout the sixteenth and seventeenth centuries cats were subjected to appalling torments . . .' The words seemed to jump out of the page.

'Is that where you've been, Ka, to Tudor or Stuart times?'

She carried on eating, she was obviously very hungry. She must have had a very narrow escape. He must stop her going again. The question was, how?

22

Chapter 4

When Chris Hope saw Ka's neck he said they must take her to the vet. He rang the university to say he would be in late. He rang St Saviour's to say Topher would be late too – and then they set off. Topher was surprised – and pleased, of course. His dad wasn't the sort to make a fuss and he hardly ever let Topher have time off school. He was an education fanatic.

Topher carried Ka in a cardboard carrier which they'd got from the vet's when she'd had her injections, when they'd first got her. She wasn't very grateful. She yowled most of the way. The vet's surgery was in Hornsey Lane. As they walked through Peace Park his dad said, 'I wonder how it happened. Poor old puss cat.'

He couldn't understand it, he said. If Ka had worn a collar, that would have explained it; she might have got it caught on a branch while climbing a tree, and then broken the skin on her neck while struggling to get free. But she didn't wear a collar.

Topher wondered too. It seemed to him that Ka had been fighting for her life last night. Something had terrified her. In the past cats often had a terrible time, even in Ancient Egyptian times when they were worshipped. Most were treated well, but some were sacrificed in religious ceremonies. He'd saved Ka from that once. Surely she hadn't gone back there again?

Mr Morris, the vet, was mystified too. He was a big hairy Scotsman. Fortunately Ka seemed to like him. He talked to her, in a soft growly burr, while he examined her, and when he'd finished he said her windpipe was bruised. It did look as if someone had tried to strangle her, or as if her head had been caught in some sort of trap. He gave her an injection, to ward off any infection, and told them to keep her in, especially at night. Then he gave them a week's supply of the antibiotic he'd injected her with, and told them they must make sure she finished the whole course. On the way home they bought some litter and a tray.

'You've got to stay at home for a whole week, Ka. At least.' Topher filled the tray with litter while his dad fixed the cat flap so that she couldn't open it. Ka wasn't impressed. She stood by the back door yowling. She hated using a litter tray. Topher filled her dishes and put them on the floor too.

Chris Hope said. 'It's all right, Ka. We won't look at you while you perform. We're off now.' He insisted that Topher went to school for the rest of the day.

By the time Topher got there it was nearly lunchtime. Fortunately he didn't have to sit down and concentrate on lessons as the whole class was busy clearing the classroom for the summer holiday. Ellie was dismantling a display on the back wall and she asked Topher to help her. It was all about the Tudors and Stuarts. Was that why he thought Ka had gone to the sixteenth or seventeenth century – just because they were in his mind? They'd done nothing about Tudor and Stuart cats, though they had them. They had rats too. They'd carried

24

the plague, but people didn't know that then. Pity. They might have treated cats better if they'd known. They'd done Henry VIII and Elizabeth I and Shakespeare and Sir Francis Drake and emptying pisspots out of the window into the street. Samuel Pepys said pisspots in his diary.

'Stop day-dreaming, Topher, and hold these.' Ellie was handing him drawing pins which she'd taken out of a life-size painting of Elizabeth I. Henry VIII was still on the wall. They'd drawn round each other to get the body shapes, then painted the clothes onto them.

'Where've you been anyway?' said Ellie.

He told her – and she was pleased that Ka was back, but very upset about her injury.

When Ellie came home with him after school, Ka was sleeping peacefully on his bed, so they left her while they went downstairs to get a snack. Then they came upstairs to eat it. After a bit Ellie said, 'Where's your little statue gone? I thought I found it again.'

He said, 'I told you. It's only there when she's time-travelling.'

And Ellie gave him a long look.

Then Ka woke up. They were eating cheese and crackers, her favourites, after all, and while she was eating bits from Topher's fingers, Ellie examined her neck. She couldn't believe it. 'What sort of maniac would have done that?'

Topher told her what the vet had said, and pointed to the museum book. He mentioned the appalling torments.

She said, 'Like what?'

He told her to read it – to herself.

When she'd finished she said, 'I suppose it's not surprising really, when you think of it. I mean Henry VIII killed two wives just because they didn't have sons for him. They were cruel people. What about that queen who burned people just because they weren't Catholics?'

'Bloody Mary?'

'Yes.' They'd laughed at that in class.

'And someone before that killed them because they *were* Catholics. They were cruel, crazy and cruel.'

'It says they killed cats because they thought they were in league with the devil, and some people celebrated Elizabeth I's coronation by burning a huge basket full of cats – alive!'

'Mwa!'

Ka had jumped off the bed and was making her way towards the stairs.

It wasn't till Ellie was going that she mentioned the time-travelling. She said, 'Do you really believe that's what Ka does, Topher?'

He said yes, and she said she'd have to think about it.

Later, he had words with Ka, while she was licking the remains of Spaghetti Bolognese off his supper plate. He said, 'You mustn't go time-travelling, Ka, it's dangerous.'

She stopped licking for a second.

'Where did you go, anyway?'

She didn't answer.

But he asked her again, when they were upstairs together in his bedroom. He was playing on his computer and she'd jumped onto his knee. Sometimes, she seemed to think he switched on the computer just for her, and

26

took delight in pawing anything that moved. It annoyed him if he wasn't in the mood, especially when she stood on the keyboard to do it, and produced a lot of gobbledygook. Once though she'd produced a word of amazing significance – the clue to her whereabouts – and it was the memory of this which prompted his question.

'Where did you go, Ka? Where did you go?'

She hesitated and then reached out with her right front paw.

He watched entranced as she picked out the letters.

R*iche mou*nt

Was that a word? Was that the name of anywhere? It wasn't a place he recognised. It looked a bit French.

'Where's that, Ka? When was that?'

She didn't answer.

He typed in another question, and after a moment's hesitation, she pressed two keys with her right paw.

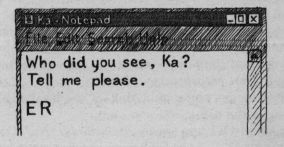

'E R' The letters were next to each other on the keyboard. Did they mean anything?

Ka looked at him severely, as if he was being very stupid.

Chapter 5

Leaving her each day to go to school – not knowing whether she'd be there when he returned – was nerve wracking. So was going to sleep and not knowing whether she'd be at the end of his bed when he woke up. But finding the stone cat – that was what he feared the most. Then he would know she was in some other time. But what could he do to prevent it? She said she'd been to *Richemount*. He'd asked his dad about that, without saying why, and his dad said it sounded a bit like Richmond which was south-west of London. On Tuesday after school Topher went to the library near the tube station, and looked it up in a dictionary of place names. And there were two Richmonds, one in London, one in Yorkshire. Henry VII, who was also the Earl of Richmond in Yorkshire, had named the London one after the Yorkshire one – and it was spelt as *Richemount* in 1502! He'd built a palace there.

When he got home after this bit of research Ka was waiting in the hall.

He said, 'Did you go to *Richemount*, Ka? Did you visit the king?' She just led him to her dish in the kitchen.

He asked her again later – burying his face in her fur – but she still didn't answer.

She was there on Wednesday, Thursday and Friday, the last day of term – and the last day of St Saviour's for Ellie and Topher. Ellie was a bit sad about that, and excited about their starting a new school in September. Topher had other things on his mind.

So far so good though. Ka seemed to sleep most of the time – on his bed. Stretched out beside her on Friday evening he said, 'I wish you'd talk more, Ka.' She talked on very rare occasions. 'I'd like to know whether you're going again. Are you?'

She still didn't answer. He stroked her neck which had healed up quickly. The fur was growing exactly the same as it had been before, dark with white flecks on the top of her neck, light gold beneath her chin but it was short like velvet and it had a velvety sheen.

On Saturday Dr Carstairs came to see them. Topher was surprised when his dad said she was coming, as he thought he'd seen the last of her. But Cambridge, where she'd moved to, wasn't far away. She came on the train and his dad met her at the station. Then they all went for lunch at a French café in Highgate. It was hot and they ate outside at a table, covered with a red and white check cloth. Topher had an omelette with chips and a Coke. The grown-ups had steaks – and red wine – and they talked to each other a lot, but in a moment's silence Topher did manage to ask Dr Carstairs if she experimented on animals – which took the smile off his dad's face. He looked as if he was about to tell Topher to shut up, but Dr Carstairs didn't seem to mind. She said she had in the past. She'd grown cancers on white mice, to find out what caused cancers to grow – because she thought it was important to know. Topher said he thought using mice was cruel. She said she thought cancer was cruel and that cats were much crueller to mice than she was, and as if to underline her point, when they got home, there was a headless mouse on the doorstep. It wasn't Ka's. She was still inside, stretched out on the cold kitchen floor, but she livened up when Dr Carstairs gave her some bits of steak that she'd brought home from the restaurant. Then she made coffee and his dad put on a record – of cello music that his mum used to like.

Topher went round to Ellie's and stayed to tea.

Ellie came on the art course which began on the following Monday. It was in Waterlow House in Highgate. Ellie called for him, shortly after his dad had gone to work and they walked there, leaving Ka inside with the cat-flap still closed, though she was so fed up with staying inside that she'd started attacking the pot plants. Topher knew he'd have to give her her freedom soon.

Ellie chose to do pottery too, though there was a choice of pottery and painting and paper sculpture, which sounded fun. In pottery they all had to put on plastic pinafores and grab a lump of clay. The tutor, called Liz, said she wanted everyone to get the feel of the clay first. They had to squeeze and pummel it till it was smooth, then roll it into snakes. Then she showed them how to make a coil pot and they all did, but she said they could all choose what to make next. When Topher said he'd like to make a model of his cat she told him to bring in some photos of her, or better still make some sketches tonight.

Unfortunately, when he got home Ka wouldn't keep still. She'd slept all day and she didn't want to sleep any more. First, she chased everything that moved – her tail, crane flies, moths – and quite a few things that didn't. When she did sit down she washed herself very thoroughly first with one leg, then another stuck in the air. She did anything except sleep. When Topher rang to tell Ellie the problem she said he'd have to cheat. She'd bring round her Cat Encyclopaedia which had hundreds of pictures of cats in it, including some diagrams of their skeletal structure. She arrived a few minutes later, but wouldn't stay. She was helping her brother with some cooking, she said. They were making sweets and if she didn't get back he'd have eaten them all.

The encyclopaedia was really useful. It explained why cats were such acrobats and why they could lick their bottoms. It was because a cat's skeleton was in two separate pieces, joined together by muscle tissue, so they could bend themselves in two. He made a few sketches from it then took it upstairs to read it in bed, and Ka came in through the bedroom door. He lifted the bedcovers and she leaped onto the bed. Then, after a lot of circling, she nestled in the curl of his stomach.

It was hot but he wanted her there. He put the book on the floor and snuggled down with her. He said, 'You won't go again, will you, Ka?'

She started to purr. *Cou... rrrse not. Cou... rrrse not.* Was that what she was saying?

'Why did you go to Richmond, Ka?'

Don't wo... rrry. Don't wo... rrry.

'You said – wrote – that you went to Richmond. Why?' She didn't answer.

He didn't sleep very well. He woke up in the early

hours with the words of a nursery rhyme on his lips, but couldn't remember the dream he'd been having.

> 'Pussy cat, pussy cat,
> Where have you been?
> I've been to London
> To visit the Queen.'

He felt a bit ashamed; it was so childish. Ka seemed to like it though. She snuggled closer and he felt her purrs against his chest – she'd moved up a bit. Praying that she would stay with him forever, he went back to sleep.

Chapter 6

The week passed quickly. His clay model of Ka worked out well. He did her curled up, mostly because that was easiest, but also because he loved the shape of her when she slept like that, an almost perfect circle, like a soft cushion. Even better though, was the real Ka, plumper now, waiting for him each evening.

On Sunday Ellie's mum invited him and his dad to a barbecue lunch and Chris Hope really enjoyed himself, talking computers with Ellie's dad and education and politics with her mum. Better still he agreed when Mrs Wentworth said she would look after Topher during the holidays. On the way home he said it was because the Wentworths were such a nice family and it was good for Topher to be with a proper family. Topher was pleased that his dad had got to know the Wentworths better. Perhaps now he wouldn't feel so lonely. Quite often he stayed for a chat if he collected Topher from the Wentworths' house. He didn't mention Dr Carstairs all that week. Things were looking up. So it was a bit of a shock when he suddenly said, 'How would you feel about moving, Topher?' It was a Thursday evening. He'd been reading the newspaper which was by the side of his chair open at the jobs page.

Topher said, 'I'd hate it, and so would Ka.' She was on his knee. 'Everyone knows that cats hate moving.

You wouldn't like that, would you, Ka?'

She didn't reply and nor did his dad. Topher carried on watching 'Animal Antics'.

Next day, when he mentioned to Ellie what his dad had said, she said, 'I shouldn't worry about it, Topher. There aren't many jobs around. Think of all the unemployment.'

But at breakfast, only a few weeks later, his dad opened his post and said he'd got an interview, for a job in Cambridge. He said he probably wouldn't get it – there had been hundreds of applicants and twelve of them were being interviewed – but they might as well both go and make a day of it. He said that Cambridge was a really interesting place and Topher could go to a museum or something while he went for the interview. Afterwards, they could go on the river if it was a nice day. Molly could join them perhaps. He was sure Topher would like Cambridge.

Topher didn't say anything. He couldn't. He couldn't believe what he was hearing. What was the point of talking about things? He'd told his dad he didn't want to move and he'd been totally ignored. 'I'd hate it.' That was what he'd said. That was what he meant, but it was obvious why his dad wanted this new job – to be near Molly Carstairs. He cared more about her than he did about his own son.

Chris Hope got the job. Of course he did. While Topher was being dragged round Cambridge by Molly, who took the day off work specially, his dad was being brilliant and impressive, beating the opposition into a cocked hat. Well, that's what Molly said, when they picked his dad up from the science park, a sort of industrial estate where P & R Computers was situated. His dad blushed – to the roots of his thinning hair – and so did Topher who was in the back of Molly's car. It was sick-making. He thought they were going to kiss, but fortunately someone in the car behind beeped them and Molly had to move off sharply. Then she had to concentrate on driving because it was the rush hour. The interview had taken all day.

Molly said she was taking them back into Cambridge, to one of her favourite places for a picnic. Topher had helped make it. He hadn't had much choice. She'd taken him to the Fitzwilliam Museum in the morning and a supermarket in the afternoon, saying it was best if he chose what he liked to eat. They'd gone back to her tiny house to put it all together. That's when she said he could carry on calling her Dr Carstairs if he liked, but if he did she'd call him Master Hope. So he didn't call her anything after that, but – it was annoying – he started to think of her as Molly. He didn't want to but he did. She introduced him to her cat who was nice – not wonderful like Ka – but a heavy male tabby called Buggins. They picnicked – in a punt on the river – and it was all very jolly, and Topher felt miserable. Molly had bought all his dad's favourite things and a bottle of champagne. On the way home, on the train, Chris Hope said, 'I've got to tell you, Topher. I'd like to marry Molly. How do you *feel* about that?'

He didn't bother to answer. What was the point? He didn't say anything all the way home. He felt that he didn't want to speak to his dad ever again – that's how he *felt*.

When he told Ellie – on the following day – she was almost as shocked as Topher was. She said, 'It's hardly worth your starting St Bede's.' That was the new secondary school they'd both chosen to go to in September, in less than a fortnight's time. 'You'll just get settled in and you'll have to go and get settled somewhere else.'

'I shan't.'

'What?'

'Get settled. I'll hate it. I won't know anybody.'

She said, 'You will make new friends.'

He didn't say anything. He wasn't that good at making friends and couldn't imagine making another as good as Ellie.

She said, 'I'll miss you, Topher.'

Mrs Wentworth found them both in the garden looking glum. When they explained she said it was a shock, but not the end of the world, and reminded Ellie of how she hadn't wanted to move to London. 'Now, you'd hate to move back up North,' she said.

'That's because I've made friends with Topher.'

'You can still keep in touch with each other. There's the phone, and letters, and you can still see each other sometimes, stay with each other even. You're always welcome here, Topher, you know that.'

She said she was sure they wouldn't be moving quickly anyway. His dad would have to give at least a month's notice to his place of work and most probably three months.

Mrs Wentworth was underestimating his dad's enthusiasm. When he came home that night he'd handed in his notice to the university, who had accepted the minimum one month because they'd been down-sizing whatever that was. He'd contacted an estate agent about selling the house. Not that he was in a great hurry to sell, he said, as they could move into Molly's house. Later, when they'd sold both houses they'd be able to buy a really nice place. On Wednesday when Topher came home from Ellie's at tea-time there was a FOR SALE notice outside. Ka was sitting by it. Topher lifted her up and carried her inside.

She let him carry her, seemed to know that he needed her close to him. When he flumped down on his bed she

stayed with him, in his arms like a baby with her legs in the air, purring, though she didn't usually like that position.

Don't wo . . . rry. Don't wo . . . rry. Don't worry.

'You won't like moving, Ka. Cats don't, do they?'

She twisted round – and he thought she was going to jump onto the floor – but she stood facing him.

Don't wo . . . rry. Don't wo . . . rry.

'You won't like living with Buggins. He's enormous. He'll eat your food.' She rubbed her cheek against his cheek, put her pink nose against his nose. 'You will come with me, won't you?' Moving without her would be unbearable.

Of cou . . . rrse. Of cou . . . rrse. Don't wo . . . rry. Don't wo . . . rry.

For a few moments he wondered if she knew something that he didn't. Perhaps it would be all right. But how could it?

Chapter 7

The next few weeks passed incredibly quickly. The new term started. Topher and Ellie started at St Bede's with Topher wearing the right uniform – he insisted – though his dad said it wasn't worth buying it. The yellow and green colour scheme was ghastly, it made Topher's pale skin look jaundiced, but the thought of a new uniform made him feel worse.

On the Friday of the first week of term his dad took him to Cambridge to look at new schools. This time he hired a car. Chris Hope had made the appointments – on Molly's advice. She'd asked friends and neighbours for their opinions, but he said it was up to Topher to make up his own mind. He could choose, so he should ask about anything he wanted to know. It didn't matter how many questions he asked.

They looked at two schools in the morning and one in the afternoon, but he felt more looked at than looking. It was excruciatingly embarrassing traipsing in and out of classrooms sandwiched between his dad and some weird teacher, and some of the teachers were very weird. His dad asked loads of questions – about homework and library provision and the number of languages they taught. The teachers never stopped talking. One went on and on about caring, then foamed at the mouth when he saw a pupil standing outside a classroom without something or other. Another went mad at a girl wearing a hat.

At the last school, they met the Head – a Scot called Mr Dundee – as they had at the other two, but after the usual chat he asked Topher if he'd like to be shown round the school by a pupil. Actually Topher didn't hear him make this offer. He was staring out of the window, trying to work out what the school uniform was, when his dad nudged him quite sharply. Mr Dundee repeated what he'd said and Topher mumbled that another pupil would be fine.

Melissa Presland, one of the older pupils, wore trousers and a long flowery shirt – it seemed there wasn't a uniform. She was fat and very talkative and she had a lot of frizzy fair hair. Fortunately she didn't seem to require him to say much, but she did ask him if he wanted to go into the classrooms, which spared him going through the being ogled at routine. Melissa took him almost everywhere else though. She took her duties very seriously. In fact she was more like a mother than a pupil; one boy actually came and told her he'd lost his trainers and she found them for him! By the time they got back to the Head's office he must have seen inside every cupboard, and while they were waiting for the Head and his dad she said the school – she called it 'the college' – hadn't got a sixth form, which meant Year 10 pupils like her got a lot of responsibility. She ran the Animal Welfare Club.

She'd shown him the AWC, as she called it, in some outbuildings. It was for anyone who liked animals, but particularly pupils who couldn't keep pets at home. They could keep them at school. He'd seen guinea pigs,

rabbits, mice and a family of Vietnamese pot-bellied pigs. She said they had talks by people like vets and RSPCA officers, and films about animals, and trips sometimes, to a rare-breeds farm most recently. When she asked Topher if he liked animals, he found himself telling her about Ka, not *all* about Ka of course, just that he was worried about losing her in the move, and not getting on with Buggins. Then he'd had to explain about Buggins belonging to Molly and she said, 'You don't like her, do you?'

He was thinking about that when she said, 'It doesn't matter. I don't like my step*father*.'

Stepmother – he hadn't thought of Molly like that.

Melissa said, 'Well, at least yours likes animals.'

She said she really loved animals and that she was thinking of becoming a vegetarian. The AWC's next event was a talk by a vegetarian. She'd pointed out posters about it as they walked round the school. She said Petra who was the club secretary thought they ought to be more active, actually do more to help animals and Petra even wondered about the ethics of keeping animals, especially in cages. She'd been down to Littleport to protest at the export of calves. Topher had wanted to when he'd seen it on the television news. He'd felt really sorry for those calves, taken from their mums at only a few days' old and crammed into lorries and transported for hundreds of miles. Nobody asked them what they wanted to do either.

He liked the sound of Petra and the AWC.

So when his dad said, 'Which one is it then?' – they were back in the car at the time, driving to Molly's house – he said, 'That'll do.'

'What'll do? Please make yourself clear, Topher. Do

42

you mean Rawlins?'

'The one we've just been to. The last one.'

'Rawlins. It's called Rawlins Community College. You liked that one? Good. I liked it too, even though the pupils looked a bit scruffy, some of the staff too. Molly said it's got a good reputation though.'

Topher said, 'I *liked* St Bede's. Rawlins will *do*.'

His dad didn't answer and he rang the school as soon as they got to Molly's house. Topher heard him asking for Mr Dundee as he stood in the small hall looking at a collection of fossils by the phone. Molly wasn't there, but she'd given his dad a key. There was a note on the kitchen table telling them to make themselves at home.

They didn't stay the night, thank goodness, though Molly, when she came home from work, showed Topher round the house. There were two spare rooms and she asked him which one he'd like. One looked over lots of back gardens, the other over a fairly grotty street, a bit like Coronation Street, though it had been brightened up with paint and window boxes. He chose the one at the front because it was furthest away from Molly's – and his dad's, of course.

The wedding was fixed for the last Saturday in September. It would take place at a London registry office, but the honeymoon wasn't till half-term, when Topher was going to stay with Ellie. That had been Mrs Wentworth's idea. According to Ellie his dad had told her mum he was going to book a holiday for the three of them. Mrs Wentworth had said, 'Why not ask Topher if he'd like to come and stay with us instead?'

Good old Mrs Wentworth! He was still worried about Ka though. How would she take to all this upheaval?

Chapter 8

Ka didn't seem to mind too much. When they all moved into Molly's house, in Lyntone Road, on the Sunday after the wedding, Topher had buttered her paws, on Molly's suggestion. It was a traditional way of getting a cat to settle into a new home, she said. Topher thought she was joking. On the other hand Ka loved butter. Molly gave him some that she'd bought specially, and he smeared some on her right front paw. She licked it tentatively, then avidly and miaowed for more.

And Buggins didn't seem to mind Ka too much. At first, when Topher brought her in, Buggins sniffed her all over, and Ka let him. Then she sniffed him all over, walking right round his considerable bulk. He just stood and let her. Then he'd walked away, from the kitchen into the sitting room, where he'd taken possession of his own squashy armchair. It was his, Molly said. He never went on her matching chair or on the sofa. He never went on her lap; she wished he was that sort of cat but he wasn't.

While Buggins slept, Ka carried on sniffing, all over the house. Topher followed at a discreet distance. She sniffed stairs, door frames, and at least one piece of furniture in every room. Then she came downstairs again, located the sleeping Buggins, strolled to the armchair opposite, rubbed it with both cheeks then sprang onto it.

Molly laughed and said, 'We'll have to sit on the sofa, won't we?' – though Ka had now climbed onto the arm of the chair.

Topher went into the garden. It was quite cold outside. There was an autumnal chill in the air and the grass was covered with yellow leaves. Through the window he could see them all – Molly and his dad close together on the sofa and the two cats in their chairs – in a circle of light from the gas-fire. Very cosy. Molly's house was comfortable he had to admit, though tiny, but she wasn't much of a gardener. Against the back fence a row of bare poplars looked like broomsticks. Some nasturtiums had gone mad, their long tendrils criss-crossing the lawn, but the only other flowers were weeds. One, called honesty he thought – also silver-penny because it was flat and round and silvery – was rampant. The smell of new-mown grass from next door suggested that the neighbours were keener.

Through a gap he could see an elderly couple pottering in the borders. From further on came the sounds of children playing and a football commentary on someone's radio.

He went into the garage to check over his bike, which he'd be using regularly now, unless Molly took him to school on her way to work. He didn't want that. Rawlins Community College was a couple of miles away. Molly said there was someone else in the street who went there. He went out for a ride round but didn't come across anyone under thirty.

On Monday morning he set off on his own. Two hours later, after a bit of hanging about, he was a member of 7Y, in Mr Young, known as Gerry-atric's class. He had shoulder-length grey hair. When Topher joined the class everyone was sitting around in groups – doing PHASE, the teacher said. They were discussing alcohol and recording their thoughts. Mr Young gave him a timetable and said he'd sort out which sets he was in later. For the time being he could go to classes with Tim Honeycutt. There was a bit of a snigger when he said this. By the time break came it was clear that Tim Honeycutt, a sporting hero type, didn't want Topher's company. He said he was off to the slips to practise and was sure Topher would get his bearings. Nobody else offered any help so, trying not to look like a hanger-on, he followed the majority into the playground.

The lay-out of the school was, he thought, a large H on two storeys, arranged in subject blocks. He consulted his timetable. Science was next. Thinking he remembered where the science block was, he set off, and couldn't help feeling a bit pleased to see Melissa Presland ahead. She was carrying a huge bag of wood shavings. Seeing him, she urged him to come with her to see the animals, and three minutes later he was introduced to Petra Daniels.

She was standing in front of a room of people wearing a SAVE THE WHALE tee-shirt like one Ellie wore. She had long hair like Ellie's too, and a similar confident manner. She wanted the names, she was saying, not just a show of hands, of everyone who had promised to come to the Vegetarian talk, and she wanted volunteers to leaflet the dining rooms on both the day before and the day of the event, because it was important to reach the Burger Brigade.

Topher signed the list of those promising to attend – Petra called it making a commitment – and that was when Melissa introduced him. She said he was a prospective new member and Petra nodded rather curtly. Topher was just thinking that she wasn't as friendly as Ellie, when the bell went and Melissa said she'd take him to the lab, but Melissa was too friendly. Fortunately he managed to get out before she could take him, because she reminded him of a large mother hen. There were a lot of year sevens bustling round her – like chicks – and he didn't want to be one of them. Maybe the AWC wasn't such a good idea. In Science he got talking to a boy called Simon who was in the Chess Club. He offered to take Topher to that. Unfortunately it was in a week's time, at the same time as the talk he'd promised to go to.

So he went to the talk which convinced him he'd be healthier – and nicer – if he didn't eat meat. There really was no need to eat animals. It was cruel. The speaker had shown a film of an abattoir. He couldn't put it out of his mind, the lovely cows queuing patiently to be slaughtered. He was thinking about it, cycling home, when Petra came alongside him, on a mountain bike with umpteen gears. She said she'd been really glad to see him at the meeting and asked him what he thought. When he told her, she said, 'What are you going to do about it then?'

He said, 'I don't know.'

It was feeble, he knew, but he didn't see how he could suddenly ask Molly and his dad to start cooking vegetarian food just for him. He'd actually have to talk to them for a start. He began to explain, but didn't get very far. Petra took off. Seconds later, she was streets ahead of him – in every possible way.

Chapter 9

'What do you think, cats? Would you like to be vegetarians?'

Ka and Buggins were waiting for him in the kitchen,
Ka on top of the tumble drier, because wherever Buggins
was, she liked to be higher. In fact he was on a heap of
newspapers under the worktop. When Ka jumped down
he slid down, onto the floor, avalanching the newspapers
in the process.

'Mwow!' Ka yowled.

Buggins just stared at Topher who opened a tin of
Rabbit Chunks, Ka's current favourite. Buggins ate anything – fast. He'd eat his own then Ka's, if he got the
chance, so Topher fed her on the surface and Buggins
on the floor. He was too fat to jump up.

'I said, would you like to be vegetarians?'

There was no need for them to answer. Even Ka, who
loved cheese and fish, loved meat too. If you didn't give
her meat she caught her own.

But there was no need for humans to eat it. They
were different. They could choose. Leaving the back
door open, so that the cats could go out – Molly hadn't
got a cat-flap – he went upstairs to read the Vegetarian
Society leaflets. By the time his dad called him down for
the evening meal he'd made up his mind.

It was Spaghetti Napolitano, Molly said, not their

usual Bolognese, but she hoped they'd like it. His dad said he was sure they would, but with a deep breath Topher pushed it aside.

'Sorry, I'm vegetarian.' There, he'd said it. He reached for the bread, fortunately nice crusty bread. Molly always bought nice bread. With thick butter it was delicious. Who needed meat? He could feel the silence round the table though, and waited for his dad to argue.

But Molly said, 'Topher. It *is* vegetarian. The sauce is made of tomatoes and onions, that's all, except herbs. You can add grated cheese if you like.'

It tasted okay, no – *be fair* – it was good. She was a good cook. So why did he feel disappointed? Later, when he and his dad were washing up, Molly said, 'If you want to be a veggie, Topher, that's fine by me.'

His dad started to disagree, but she waved him down. 'No, really, it's no trouble. I do a lot of vegetarian dishes anyway, more when I lived on my own. It's healthier. The latest research says so. Everybody should have at least five portions of fruit or veg per day and a much lower fat intake, especially animal fat.'

His dad said he didn't mind eating some vegetarian food, as long as he could still eat fish, and he would like to eat red meat sometimes. And bacon, he couldn't do without the occasional bacon sandwich and . . . He stopped because Molly was laughing.

She said, 'Point taken. You don't want to become a vegetarian. Topher does, and I'm inclining that way.'

His dad said, 'Won't that mean a lot of extra work?'

She said, 'Not if Topher does some cooking too. How do you feel about it, Topher? If you could cook the occasional meal it would be great, especially when we're late home.'

Next day she came home with two cookery books; *Real Fast Food* which had a lot of vegetarian recipes in it and *Italian Vegetarian Cookery*. That night Topher cooked Spicy Potatoes with Peppers and everyone declared it a triumph, even Ka. Especially Ka. Probably because it had a topping of melted cheese. She purred ecstatically all evening, and followed him up to bed, still purring.

Of all the rooms in the house she liked his best. So did he, probably because it was full of familiar things. He'd brought his furniture and everything else from his old bedroom, everything except the little statue because he couldn't find it, thank goodness. Because he had Ka.

'And you're staying, aren't you?'

She looked as if she were, curled up beneath the bedclothes.

Don't wo . . . rry. Don't wo . . . ry. With her warm fur against his skin, he didn't need a hot water bottle, even if the nights were getting chilly.

At Animal Welfare Club on Monday, when Petra asked how many members had decided to become vegetarians, he put up his hand. She caught up with him on the way home from school to say how pleased she was.

She said, 'How did you do it? Persuade your mum, I mean.'

He muttered about it not being his mum, then said, 'Oh, I just told her.' What a hero!

She said, 'Well *done*!' and when he said he was doing some of the cooking too she sounded even more impressed. He said he wished he could persuade the cats to go vegetarian, but they were convinced carnivores. Even fat Buggins brought in a bird about once a week.

Petra came home with him, because she wanted to see Ka, she said. He let them both in through the back door. She greeted the cats fondly, but wandered off when Topher started opening a tin to feed them. When she reappeared she had the post with her and said, 'Who's the scientist then?'

'My stepmother. Why?'

She was looking at a copy of *New Scientist* which came every week. Through the plastic envelope he saw the headline TIME TRAVEL PROVED, and for a moment he forgot Petra.

'What sort of scientist? Does she experiment on animals?'

He heard someone's key in the front door.

Petra went on, 'She does, doesn't she? Gosh, I can see why you don't like her. Melissa said you didn't get on.'

And Molly walked in. She said, 'Hello,' then went upstairs – to change, she said – and Topher felt himself going red all over. Had Molly heard? She looked upset.

Petra said, 'Don't worry about it. These people ought to know what people think.'

What did he think? He didn't know, that was the trouble.

Later there was a bit on the news about animal rights activists. They were stepping up their campaign to stop testing on animals. A researcher had been injured by a letter bomb. Molly knew the man. Martin somebody. She said he was doing important work on cystic fibrosis, which killed hundreds of children each year.

His dad said, 'Be careful, darling. We must all be careful. We must check the post and check the cars before we get into them.'

She said, 'Don't worry.'

He said, 'I can't help worrying. We must be all be on our guard.'

Molly said, 'We should speak out, put the issues before people. Most people want cures for cancer and cerebral palsy and Aids and all the diseases that cause suffering and ruin lives. If that means some animals die in the process, well . . .' Stroking Buggins, she said, 'They tried to kill Martin because he experimented on a few *mice*. What do you think about that?'

Topher still didn't know what to think. He went to bed with the *New Scientist* magazine. He wanted to read the article about time travel.

Ka followed him upstairs and headed straight for the red beanbag that Molly had given Topher as a moving-in present. As she trampled the beans into submission he flumped down beside her. The article began: 'TIME TRAVEL PROVED' but it was a bit misleading. It said that physicists had 'resolved the conundrum that had Einstein and the others floundering'. But it didn't say how. The conundrum was this. What if you travelled back in time and altered something? Killed your granny for instance? Wouldn't you take yourself out of existence too? If you had, how could you be time-travelling? It *said* scientists had solved this 'by applying the principle of least action to a mathematical model', and that time travel was 'only possible under conditions in which a time traveller cannot collide with himself'. But they were still asking how that could be brought about.

Topher said, 'Shall we tell them, Ka? I bet they wouldn't believe us.'

But she was asleep, purring like a motor mower.

Next day Petra brought some vegetarian cat food to school and she came round after school to see the cats' reaction. Buggins did take it. Ka didn't. Petra suggested mixing it with her tinned food and as they watched her sniffing it suspiciously, Petra said, 'Where did you say your stepmother worked?'

'At the university.'

'Yes, but where?'

'I'm not sure.'

Ka was eating now, very tentatively, from the edge of the dish.

And Petra said, 'Do you think you could find out?'

Ka stopped eating and Petra stroked her back. 'Does she work in the ARL?'

'I don't know. Why?'

'They do terrible things there.'

What had Molly said? They do mostly tissue culture.

54

They do as few animal experiments as possible.

He said so and Petra exploded. Ka shot into the hall. 'They do thousands each year! And that's only the *authorised* ones we know about!'

He couldn't think of anything to say.

She thrust something in front of him. 'Look.'

It was a photograph of a cat with things stuck into its head. 'Electrodes! That's what they are! And that's not the worst. Do you want to see any more?' She had a sheaf of photographs.

He shook his head. And she left, slamming the door behind her.

Next day she said, 'Sorry I lost my temper yesterday. It's just that I feel so strongly about cruelty.' She'd come to his classroom again, first thing, and he felt embarrassed and ashamed, embarrassed because others were watching, ashamed because he felt embarrassed. She said, 'I *can't* stand around and let these things go on.'

Quite a few people were listening.

She said, 'It makes me angry when people don't want to know.'

He didn't want to know.

She said, 'I'll leave these with you. The rest of you can look if you like.' Out of the corner of his eye he could see her photographs being passed from one person to another and he could hear gasps and shudders.

Simon Mason said, 'How do we know these photographs are genuine?'

Petra said, 'They are, but you've got a point. What we really need are photographs of things which happen locally.'

Before she left, as Gerry-atric appeared, she said to Topher, 'You could help with that, of course, if you wanted to.'

On Monday several people from his class turned up at the AWC in the dinner hour.

That night Ellie phoned to say half-term was only three weeks away and she was looking forward to seeing him. She asked if Ka was coming. He said he wasn't sure. He'd like to bring her, but it might unsettle her. She could stay with Buggins and be looked after by a neighbour.

Ellie said, 'What did you say Molly's cat was called?'

She laughed when he told her. He'd forgotten her cat was called Muggins. She said, 'Maybe you should bring Buggins as well.' They talked about names for a bit – and their new schools. She said one of her teachers was called Micro Bottom, because his name was Mike Rowbotham, and Topher told her about Gerry-atric and Mr Dundee who was called Fruitcake. Then Ellie said she was in the top set for English and he said he was finding the maths a bit tough. Molly was helping him in the evenings though.

Ellie said, 'What's she like, as a teacher I mean?' and he said, 'Okay,' because she was. She didn't say, 'Oh you *must* know this, Topher,' when it was clear he didn't.

Then Topher told Ellie about becoming a vegetarian because he thought her mum should know.

Before he went to bed he asked Molly what she was going to do with Buggins when she and his dad went on holiday. He didn't say honeymoon, it sounded daft. She said she was going to book him into the cattery and she would book for Ka if he wanted her to go there. He said he'd like to take her to Ellie's really. Molly said she thought that would be okay. She had never seen a cat so attached to a person as Ka was to Topher. She was sure she wouldn't get lost or anything.

Next day his dad fixed a cat-flap. They all thought it was safe to let Ka come and go as she pleased now. For the next few nights she went out, but Topher always found her on his bed when he woke up in the morning. But on Friday morning she wasn't there. She wasn't there when he came home from school.

It was the beginning of things going wrong.

Chapter 10

It was a miserable weekend. Ka didn't come home and on Saturday morning Molly got a threatening letter, telling her to leave her job or be prepared to suffer like the animals she tortured. It wasn't signed. She was upset and said, 'I don't torture animals. We treat the laboratory animals very well.' His dad was furious. Topher had never seen him so angry. He said, 'These people are cowards. Anonymous letters! They haven't even got the courage of their convictions. They hate people more than they like animals – that's their problem!'

On Monday evening when Molly came home from work Ka still wasn't home. After tea, Molly suggested taking a photo of Ka round all the neighbours and asking

them if they'd seen her. She said she'd come too. They went to every house in the road and in the road whose gardens backed onto theirs, but nobody could remember seeing her.

The only good thing was that the little statue didn't turn up.

Next day at animal club Topher told Petra and Melissa about Ka's absence.

Petra said, 'Are you really so surprised?'

He wasn't sure what she meant, till Melissa said, 'You're not saying Topher's stepmother took his cat, are you?'

When Petra didn't reply, he thought perhaps she was. He was sure she was wrong about that, but when he got home he went into Molly's study. What exactly did she do? Her books and papers didn't tell him much. They were mostly full of chemical formulae and diagrams. The only photos were of himself, which surprised him a bit, and of his dad and of two other little girls. He couldn't help noticing two letters, addressed to Dr M. Carstairs, ARL Unit 3, Pulvers Road, Cambridge. When he saw Petra next day – she was in the dinner queue with Melissa – the address came into his head though he hadn't tried to remember it. Both girls were furious because the Head had asked them to postpone their next talk, by someone from the Anti-Vivisection Society. Stupid Old Fruitcake – to quote Petra – wanted them to re-arrange the event in the form of a debate so that people could hear both sides.

'Both sides!' Petra's clear voice attracted a lot of listeners. 'You're either for animals or against them. If you're for them, you can't possibly be for experiments on them. Animals have rights!'

Melissa said, 'I think it's because of that letter bomb.'

Simon Mason said he thought human rights were more important than animal rights.

Someone else said, 'What about all the people starving?'

Petra snapped, 'People can speak up for themselves. Animals can't. Someone has to speak up for them!' Then she left the dining room saying she was too upset to eat anything.

Topher, who couldn't avoid sitting with Melissa and her clutch of admirers, found that she wasn't as angry as Petra. She said she'd quite like to hear the other side herself.

A little kid called Sandy said, 'How's Peter, Lissa?'

Peter, it seemed, was Melissa's brother, and one of the reasons she'd like to hear the other side of the argument. If scientists could find a cure for Peter she'd be really glad. He had cystic fibrosis. It meant that there was something wrong with his lungs and he'd die – quite soon – if no one found a cure. He was only nineteen and no one with cystic fibrosis had ever lived to be more than 29. He suffered a lot. It was one of the illnesses that Molly had mentioned.

In fact the talk went ahead – in the drama studio where there was a black-out because the speaker had slides to show. Fruitcake said he'd arranged a talk about the reasons *for* testing on animals, for a week later. Ms Thompson, from the Anti-Vivisection Society, wasn't at all like Topher thought she'd be. He supposed afterwards that he'd expected another Petra, but she was as pale as

Petra was dark, as quiet as Petra was noisy. Everyone had to listen hard to hear her properly. She said she was sure there was no need to prove to people like them that testing on animals was cruel. She didn't want to upset them by showing them any more gruesome photographs. Besides, most people who thought it was cruel, also thought it was necessary. She wanted to prove that it *wasn't*. She had facts to prove it. Pointing to a graph on the screen in front of them she said that in 1849, *16,000* Londoners had died of cholera, but ten years later, in 1859, *hardly anyone* in London died of cholera.

'Now,' she asked them. 'Why was this? Why was there no cholera in 1859?'

No one answered. Then someone said something about penicillin.

She said that wasn't discovered till the twentieth century. Then she said that cholera had been virtually eradicated, not by drugs tested on animals, but by the introduction of a proper sewer system for London and better houses for the people.

'Cholera was caused by dirty water,' she said. 'When people had clean water cholera subsided.' She held up a history book, one they used in class, and read from it. 'Improved hygiene and better living conditions probably saved more lives than any medical advances.'

She waited for them to take this in, then she showed them more graphs showing that the major fatal diseases of the nineteenth century – cholera, typhus and tuberculosis – had all been overcome *before* the drugs which claimed to have cured them, had been developed.

'And yet we – in the twentieth century – go on making animals suffer,' she concluded when the lights were on again. 'We kill animals. Why?' She sat down, next to a thin young man with red hair and pale eyelashes.

Petra got up and thanked her. Then Fruitcake, who had been sitting at the back, said he hoped everyone would turn up for Dr Mark's talk next Wednesday. He reminded them that Ms Thompson had said – 'Improved hygiene and better living conditions *probably* saved more lives than any medical advances.' There was another side and he'd like them to consider it.

Afterwards Petra introduced Topher to Ms Thompson and the young man with pale lashes, who was called Ric. She said, 'This is Topher. His stepmother works in medical research – and his cat's disappeared.'

The thin young man said, 'Where exactly does she work?' Topher didn't say anything though the address was in his mouth.

The young man said quietly, 'If I knew I could get inside and have a look round. Take a few photographs. And a plan of the building would be useful.'

Petra said, 'Jenny and Ric aren't into violence, Topher.'

Ric said, 'I'm a photographer. I like to give people the facts, that's all. If your cat's in there I'd see.'

The bell rang. Topher went to lessons.

At the end of the afternoon he hurried home willing Ka to be there.

Chapter 11

She wasn't there. She'd been missing for a whole week now. He rang Ellie just in case Ka had gone back to London, because he'd heard of cats going back to their old homes. Ellie said she'd go round and have a look. She rang back later. No luck, but she'd asked the neighbours to keep a lookout and she said she'd go round every day.

On Saturday morning Molly got another anonymous letter. His dad was reading it when Topher came down for breakfast and he said, 'I hope you're careful what you say outside these walls, Topher.' There was a newsletter from school on the table. Molly was reading it. His dad, who had obviously read it earlier said, 'What did this lot have to say to your AWC?'

By 'this lot' he meant the Anti-Vivisectionists, and he was angry that they'd been invited to the school. When Topher told them what Ms Thompson had said his dad was scornful. Molly was a bit fairer. She said that improved living conditions and proper sewage works had made a huge difference to people's health, but those things alone hadn't wiped out diseases. Tuberculosis for instance, which used to kill thousands of people, had only been brought under control by a drug called Streptomycin. That was a scientific success story.

'And what about inherited diseases, like cystic

fibrosis?' his dad said. 'They're not caused through a lack of hygiene. That's carried in the genes.'

Topher thought about Melissa's brother.

After breakfast his dad went and phoned the police to tell them about the letter.

Later, when Petra came round, Topher saw him locking Molly's study door. He knew she was secretary of the AWC, and now he thought it was an extremist group. But Petra had come round to help him look for Ka. They spent the morning searching the neighbourhood and putting LOST CAT notices in all the shop windows. Molly invited Petra to stay for lunch, but she said no thanks, even when Molly said it was vegetarian. On the way out Petra tried to open the study door for Buggins who was scratching at the handle. When it didn't open she didn't say anything but Topher could guess what she was thinking. He said he couldn't imagine Molly being cruel to animals.

She said he wouldn't have to imagine, if they had proof. Then she said sorry and agreed that Molly seemed nice. Proof was what they needed. They wouldn't know till they got into her lab. If Ric could get inside and take some photographs, they'd know for sure. She said, Ric wasn't into violence, he wouldn't hurt a fly, literally; he was the gentlest person she'd ever met – and if he did happen to find Ka he'd rescue her, he really would.

When she'd gone Topher thought about what she'd said. He could help, so why didn't he want to? Because he was a wimp? He knew the address of Molly's lab and he was sure there was a plan of the building in her study. Perhaps he should ring Petra and tell her he could help?

But he couldn't if the study was locked. He was glad the study was locked. But what if Ka was inside the laboratory?

Molly wouldn't have taken her – he was sure of that – but someone else might have.

Over lunch the atmosphere was frosty. His dad said pointedly that *some* people were blaming scientists for all society's ills. Molly and people like her were being persecuted like the witches of old. Molly said there was another side. Some people thought scientists were gods with magical solutions to all society's problems. They could feed the hungry, house the homeless and cure the sick.

'The trouble is that when we can't – though we do come up with solutions from time to time – we get the blame.'

'Yes, like witches, that's what I said,' his dad snapped. 'When they were curing people with their old remedies, that was fine. When things went wrong – quick, into the fire with them! People always like to blame someone else.'

It wasn't a row but the atmosphere was uncomfortable. Then, on the lunchtime news the Prime Minister said that children should be taught the difference between right and wrong. That provoked more discussion. Topher went out for a bike-ride and a think. What was right and what was wrong? Was cruelty wrong, or was it right sometimes?

When he came back Molly and his dad were tidying the garden and re-planting the catmint they'd brought from the London house. His dad, seeing him, said a cup of

65

tea would be welcome. On the way in to make one, he noticed the study door open. It didn't take him long to find a plan and fold it up small. He'd decide what to do with it later.

The kitchen was warm. Molly had been cooking cakes. When she came in to get the tea she said they were eating early because they were going out to a film – the three of them. She'd taken the liberty of booking him a ticket. It was for 'The Indian in the Cupboard' which he'd been wanting to see. She also said that Petra had rung and left her number and wanted Topher to ring back. He rang and Petra invited him to her house. When he said he couldn't she sounded really disappointed and he found himself saying that he'd leave what she wanted in a milk bottle on the doorstep.

The film was good and it was a nice evening. They bought fish and chips on the way home and ate them at home in front of the fire with Buggins in close attendance. Topher went to bed longing for Ka.

His dad woke him in the middle of the night. He was taking Molly into work, he said. Someone had broken into the lab. The police had called them. Molly wanted to go by herself, but he didn't like her doing that. Did Topher want to come with them in the car or did he mind staying on his own for a while? Topher was half asleep. He certainly didn't feel like getting up. He told his dad to go and heard a car starting up.

Then he heard an explosion.

A flash illuminated every inch of his room. Then it darkened and he crouched in his bed listening to a roaring and a hissing from outside, watching the flickering shadows on the walls. He crawled to the end of his bed to look out of the window, but couldn't see much. The glass was crazed, blurring the image of the fire below. In the orange flames he saw the silhouette of a car.

A voice said, 'It's Molly's car. Where is she?'

Where was she? Where was his dad? He couldn't see them. All he could see were flames. In the haze he could hear screams and see people in huddles.

No, no, no. This wasn't happening. It was a film. He could turn it off.

Someone yelled, 'Stand back!'

Whoosh! There was another explosion of blue and yellow flames.

'The petrol tank!'

He could smell petrol.

A siren wailed.

People were running.

It was happening. It couldn't be . . . but it was.

The siren wail came closer. A blue light flashed and an engine roared.

A fire engine screeched to a halt outside a house further up the road.

An ambulance entered the street.

'What have I done, Ka?'

What had he done? Feeling sick and dreadfully to blame, he turned to where he'd seen her – the stone Ka not the living one – because he had seen her, briefly, when the explosion lit up his room. The statue had been in the corner, peeping out from behind the red beanbag. But it was dark in his room now. He felt for the switch of his bedside lamp. It wasn't there, the lamp wasn't there. The force of the explosion must have blasted it onto the floor.

'Ka! Help me, Ka!' He wanted to see her eyes glowing in the darkness. He wanted to see her coming to life. He needed her. He needed her more than he'd ever needed her before. Staggering to the door, he found the switch to the main light, but when he pressed it nothing happened. Then his room lit up with a disco brightness. It was the lights outside. Flashing lights – blue, red and orange.

From outside too came urgent voices, running feet and slamming doors. He didn't look, couldn't bear to, but he found the statue and picked it up.

'Come back to me, Ka.'

Cradling it in his hands, he crawled back to the bedside table where it used to stand.

'I need you, Ka.' Reaching up, he placed her carefully on the table and the light shone through her large translucent ears.

'You're all I've got now.' She gleamed. But it was a trick. She was bathed in light from the road outside. From the lights of police cars and a fire engine.

The statue was lifeless. Ka was miles away. Aeons.

'I want to be with you, Ka. Wherever you are.'

It went darker. He heard a vehicle driving off. The voices outside were quieter.

He pulled back the curtain to get more light and there was a black shape – looking down at him. It was on the window-sill outside, a large black bird with round yellow eyes. A huge beak looked ready to stab him, as if he were a fieldmouse, and he felt like a fieldmouse, he felt tiny, because he *was* tiny, not much bigger than a mouse in fact. So it was happening again.

He was going to find Ka.

His transport awaited him.

Carefully, with his hand in a sheet, he made a hole in the glass and climbed through onto the outer sill. The bird, a raven he thought, turned so that its tail was by his side, a steep ramp leading up to its back. As he clambered up, he slipped a bit on the shiny feathers, and the bird peered over its shoulder. Round eyes looked critically and he tried harder, clung harder, till at last he was in the dip of the bird's curved back. Now it was looking straight ahead, but it began to move its head from side to side and back again, taking bearings, measuring dimensions as yet unfathomed by man.

Glancing down, Topher wished he hadn't, as he saw ambulance men carrying a covered body on a stretcher. Firemen were still dousing flames with foam which filled the street like snow.

He felt glad when wings suddenly rose on either side of him and the bird tensed for take-off, when he felt a gathering of energy below and a rush of air above, when with flapping wings the bird launched itself into the night air and soared with a swiftness that took his breath away. He gripped the shiny feathers as landmarks appeared and disappeared.

With astonishing speed the flood-lit Kings College, the Round Church tower, the Granby Street car park, the railway station and a stretch of illuminated track came into view and vanished. Then as they soared higher, buildings he couldn't recognise passed beneath him and boundaries blurred, fields faded and soon all he could see were tiny dots of lights, and even those vanished as

the bird's velocity increased. Then the only lights he could see were those ahead of him – stars.

Topher Hope, on a raven's back, was travelling faster than the speed of light on another journey through time.

* * *

He wasn't as afraid as last time. Then, after the first exhilaration, he'd worried about all sorts of things. What did going back in time entail? Becoming younger? Becoming a baby again? Becoming an egg, a sperm, or horror of horrors becoming nothing at all?

He'd worried that he might never return. Now, he didn't care. Getting away was all that mattered – and finding Ka.

Was she in Richemount in the sixteenth century? Then his journey wouldn't take as long as last time. Last time, he'd travelled three thousand years into the past. This time, he'd be travelling a mere three hundred or so. How long would that take? There was no means of telling.

All around him was nothingness. The stars seemed as far away as ever.

But he was leaving the Earth's surface, he knew that, to re-enter it again at some other time. That's what had happened before.

Whoosh! Whoosh!

As the bird's wings rose and fell on either side of him with mesmerising regularity, he wondered *who* he'd be this time. Whose identity would he take on? Three thousand years ago he'd been Topher, an Egyptian boy whose mother was a priestess. Who was he three hundred years ago?

Up and down went the bird's wings.

Up and down.

Up and down.

Soundlessly now as they seemed to be passing through a vacuum.

Then something passed him trailing fire.

Up and down went the wings.

Up and down.

Up and down.

Lulling him. His eyelids grew heavy. He had to close his eyes for a moment, rest his head on the bird's downy back – but he must have slept because when he woke up he felt something hard beneath him, not feathers but a wooden floor. He opened his eyes then closed them again to shut out the glare because he was in a room of brilliant colour and dazzling brightness.

Chapter 12

The dazzle was the sun's rays streaming through the diamond-panes of a small window. Mirrors reflected their light and the jewel colours of pictures on the walls. There were lots of pictures, maps mostly, but tapestries too, and lots of mirrors bouncing light and colour – and his reflection! – from one side of the attic room to another. Yes! There were a dozen or so Tophers! – though it was an instant before he recognised himself. His new clothes deceived him – puffy blue breeches, the tight-fitting doublet and the uncomfortable ruff round his neck. He stretched – holding his head so straight made his neck ache,

'Topher, what are you doing in here?'

A tall man, with a white beard – and a deep lilting voice that didn't match his appearance – was standing near the window. He wore an old-fashioned black gown but there was a frilly ruff round his neck too.

'I came to look for Ka, then I saw the globe, Father.'

That was on an oak table by his side; made of leather, it balanced in a frame showing the new lines of latitude and longitude which were such a help to sailors. It showed too the New Found Lands on the other side of the Ocean Sea.

'Where will Captain Drake be by now?' The famous sailor had consulted his father before he set off – to sail right round the world!

'In the south . . .' But the doctor stopped. 'No, child. I have been summoned. It would not do to be late.' He glanced out of the window and Topher guessed he had been communicating with Queen Elizabeth in Richemount Palace. They signalled to each other with mirrors – though they didn't know he knew that – for his father, the brilliant Doctor Dee, was also the Queen's Intelligencer. He gathered information for her, from all over the world, from the many travellers who came to the house, and by using the instruments he had invented.

'What does Her Majesty want, Father?'

'She did not say. It could be the toothache. It . . .' But the doctor broke off again, clipping Topher round the ear. 'How do you know that, forward boy?' He moved to the door. 'Goody Faldo! Find the boy something useful to do!'

'I *am* doing something useful. I'm looking for Ka,' said Topher, now looking under a table as a red-faced old woman arrived at the door, her white wimple-cap askew.

'You and that cat, Master Dee,' she huffed. 'You'll have us all burned for witchcraft.'

'See how the ignorant speak, Father.'

Now Goody Faldo went to clip him, but fortunately couldn't reach – she couldn't get in the room, her kirtle was too wide – and the doctor, gathering rolls of parchment together, said, 'It would indeed be unfortunate if the mob got hold of the cat, Goody Faldo. The boy can come with me. I think I know where the cat is.'

Fortunately, his father liked Ka nearly as much as he did, *and* he was good at finding things, *and* curing things, *and* making things – he'd made Topher a toy beetle that *moved* once! No wonder the Queen consulted him! And now he, Topher, was going to see her! He had seen her once before, so people said. She'd called at their house the day his mother died, but he'd been a baby then.

'I'm taking you to fetch Ka, boy, but Her Majesty has not seen you since you were breeched and may like to see you again. Are you properly dressed?'

'Yes, Father.' Topher felt proud of the manly clothes he'd worn since he started school. Till then he'd worn a shift like a girl!

'Let us be gone, then!' Doctor Dee swept out of the door and down the stairs – he moved quite fast for an elderly man – and Goody Faldo, already down, was standing at the bottom holding their hats. As they put them on and checked their reflections in a handmirror, she opened the door into the narrow village street.

They had to pause for a hay-cart to pass. Mistress Pottle, coming out of her house opposite, had to pause too. She wished them good day and thanked God for the good weather and his father returned her sentiments, for when it rained the street was a stream of mud. Then his father set off again, and Topher ran to keep up, staying under the eaves as far as he could, for people often missed the centre ditch when they threw their rubbish out of the window. He didn't want something disgusting landing on his head, so he kept a good lookout – and for Ka, of course. There were a few dogs mooching around, and horses, of course, and a boy was leading an ox to the common, but he only saw one cat fleetingly – most had the sense to stay out of sight. From time to time witch-fever swept through the land – and then cats and some people were in terrible danger. Nobody was safe – his own father had been put in the Tower for witchcraft in Bloody Mary's reign. Fortunately he'd been released, even though Ka visited him while he was in the Tower! She really had!

Where was she?

'Topher, cease your day-dreams!' His father was standing by a wicket gate.

'Aren't we going by boat, Father?' A road to the right led down to the river – the Thames which flowed by their house – he could see masts and sails.

'No. We can make better speed through the park.' It was ahead of them, beyond the gate, with deer drifting through the trees.

'But Ka may have gone to see the boatmen. They treat her so well.'

'Boy, make haste!' His father was inside the park now. 'Her Majesty does not like waiting.'

Suddenly Topher felt nervous.

'What shall I say to Her Majesty, Father?'

'Nothing, till she speaks to you, then bow low. Pray you, Topher, be not forward. We do not want to end up in the Tower!'

Was his father jesting? For the rest of the journey he kept pace, till he saw the red on white of the royal flags, and the rose and the golden lions of England, fluttering from the red-brick turrets of the royal palace. Richemount! The palace of Richemount! Truly a mountain of richness! He had seen it before of course but never, never had he been inside it. Its chimneys were higher than anything in Mortlake village, except possibly the church steeple, but this building was much fancier than the church – and it was built of bricks not old-fashioned stone, or wood or wattle and daub – like the village houses. This building was made of thousands and thousands of tiny bricks arranged in all sorts of intricate patterns – chequers and zig-zags and diamonds – and the mullioned windows all had diamond-shaped panes and the wrought iron gates in front of him were an incredible mixture of flowers and leaves and lions and the Queen's initials. With a finger he traced the curlicue letters – *ER ER ER* Was he really going inside? What would Elizabeth Regina be like?

'Topher!' Dr Dee was already inside on the gravel path, let past by the soldiers at the gate – resplendent in red and gold – who obviously knew him well. Now he stood, head bowed, beneath a rose-covered pergola, edged with lavender and as Topher ran to catch up the scent wafted up to his nostrils. Then, when they were yards from the door, he nearly ran into his father – would have if he hadn't skidded past him – because his father stopped suddenly when a young woman came running out of the palace entrance. And his father *beamed*. He went red, he really did. Then, when the young lady came up to them, he kissed her hand and introduced her. She was Jane Fromond, he said, lady-in-waiting to Lady Howard, one of the Queen's household.

'Doctor Dee and Master Dee!' Jane Fromond had a round smiley face, and wore a dress the colour of the lavender surrounding them. 'Her Majesty is expecting you, Doctor Dee. I am to take you to her directly.'

As she led them into the palace, her dress bobbed from side to side and brushed the gravel, and then the

flagged hallway, and then the polished wood of a wide
curving staircase – at the top of which were some double
doors, which opened as if by magic. And then they were
in a long wainscotted room at the end of which, on a
canopied dais, he could see a throne – and sitting on it,
surrounded by courtiers, was Queen Elizabeth of
England.

She had red hair and a white face – which matched her
dress! That was his first thought and he was glad no
one knew it. He felt sure you were supposed to think
something far more flattering, that she was the most
beautiful person he'd ever seen, something like that. She

wasn't – Jane Fromond was prettier – but she was the most splendid. Her ruff was enormous. She had set the fashion for ruffs, but no one was allowed to have one bigger. Hers spread out on either side of her – like a peacock's tail – framing her white face and red hair, her mountain of hair, piled high on her head so that she looked even taller than she was. And she was very tall even sitting down.

And she glittered! Her dress was stiff and crusty with gold embroidery and garnets and rubies and hundreds of creamy pearls, and there were more jewels in her hair and on her hands, and when his father went down on his knees to kiss her hand Topher saw that even her shoes glittered. Yet she was always complaining that she was short of money – his father said so – she was always wanting more money for the royal coffers.

'Your Majesty.' His father stayed low – it seemed like ages – till the Queen told him to rise.

Then before he was upright again, she started to speak – loudly – in a shrill, *sudden* voice.

'We are well pleased to see Doctor Dee. We do not know which way to turn. Our senior advisers give us contrary advice.'

Topher thought they must be the two elderly men – even older than his father – who stood behind the throne in long velvet gowns. Indicating one then the other, she said, 'Lord Burghley says we need not worry ourselves about a Spanish invasion. Sir Francis Walsingham says we should.'

She raised her hands in a gesture of despair, then smiled and turned back to his father.

'So what do you say, our map-making magician, our astrological physician, our treasure-seeking geographer? What have you seen in your magical mirrors, Welsh wizard? What have you divined with your magic rods?'

His father didn't answer. Topher thought he looked uncomfortable, and the Queen must have thought so too, because she suddenly clapped her hands and said quite softly, 'Ah, you need our ear alone.'

Then the whole court started to shuffle away from her – backwards – and Topher was wondering if he could do this and where he would go, when he realised that the Queen was addressing him.

'Master Dee.' She held out her hand, and prodded by Jane, he stumbled forward and kissed the jewelled hand as his father had done. It smelt of honeysuckle and oranges.

'Your Majesty,' he remembered to say and stayed on his knee till she told him to rise.

Then he heard her say, 'We hear you have lost something.'

In his confusion he couldn't think what she meant.

'Fortunately,' she said, 'your clever father has divined her whereabouts. But can you divine it, Master Dee, can you? Are you as clever as your father?'

Topher was too befuddled to think straight.

She laughed and called over a young courtier, who had lingered by the door. 'Sir Philip, give Master Dee a clue!'

The young man, in red velvet from head to toe, except for the lace ruff at his neck, plucked the strings of the lute in his hand, then began to sing, 'Pussy cat, pussy cat . . .'

Then of course Topher remembered!

'Where have you *been*? . . .' Sir Philip continued and the Queen laughed.

'I've been to Richemount
To visit the *Queen*!'

He finished with a ripple of notes and the Queen clapped her hands, standing now.

Topher scanned the room.

The Queen said, 'More! More! The boy needs another clue!' – and of course Sir Philip obeyed.

'Pussy cat, pussy cat
What did you *there* . . .?

I frightened a mousiekin . . . under the *chair*!' Sir Philip finished with a flourish.

'Look under the chair, Master Dee! Look under the royal chair!' laughed the Queen.

Did she mean the throne? It seemed that she did, because she stepped aside, and when he kneeled to look beneath it, there curled in a ball was Ka! He lifted her into his arms and the Queen scratched her between the ears with a ringed finger.

'Now, Jane, take them to the elephant room, and treat them well! 'Tis well that you three get on.'

What did she mean? She spoke in riddles.

As he followed Jane out of the room he heard his father say, 'My magic is of Mathematics and Measurement for the most part, Your Majesty. It is Natural Magic and Mechanical Magic . . .'

She replied, 'Then measure the meaning of last year's comet, Doctor Dee. Did it mean good or ill for our realm? Is Captain Drake filling our coffers with Spanish gold or has he gone to join his Maker?'

Chapter 13

What did the Queen mean – the elephant room? What did she mean by – "'Tis well that you three get on?'

He got his answer to the first question at least, when Jane opened a door at the bottom of the curving staircase, for in the room they entered, on the wall opposite them was a colourful tapestry of two magnificent elephants with the goddess Diana. Topher was delighted to recognise the two men studying it, even before they turned round to greet him. And John Hawkins and Martin Frobisher, two sailors who had consulted his father many times, were delighted to see him – and Ka. Sailors thought cats were lucky especially on board ship. Hawkins shook Topher's hand vigorously and he stroked Ka between the ears, but Frobisher kept his gloved hands to himself. He had only recently returned from a voyage to the Northernmost Lands and his fingers were badly frost bitten.

In black brocade edged with fur, Hawkins, now Treasurer of the Navy, looked distinguished in his courtier clothes. Frobisher seemed uncomfortable in his – as if he'd rather be back at sea – and his leather doublet, the colour of honey, looked too big for him.

Jane said, 'Tell us about your voyage, Martin.' She patted the bench beside her and Ka jumped onto it. 'Tell Topher about these – what did you call them – Eskimo?'

She turned to Topher who was standing as straight as he could with his hand on his hip, like the two sailors. 'They were creatures, so covered with fur, that they could not be sure if they were men or beasts!'

'Oh! They were men all right,' said Frobisher, 'for they tried to stop us landing.'

It took Topher a few moments to tune in to his Yorkshire speech.

'But they were covered with fur,' he went on. 'They lived in 'ouses of fur – the fur of 'uge white bears – and they ate ice 'ard frozen as pleasantly as you eat sweetmeats.' As he spoke he delved into a pouch and brought out a lump of black rock which he handed to Topher. It had a thread of gold running through it! He couldn't wait to get back, he said, to find more of the stuff, and see if the sea he'd discovered really did lead to China.

'Though he doesn't know if it's really gold yet, and he's called the sea Frobisher Straits already! It may well be a dead end! And talking of sweetmeats . . .' Hawkins laughed as a servant boy came in with a wooden trencher. 'Marchpane I do believe!' The little cakes tasting of honey and almonds were delicious. Frobisher, despite his sore fingers, fed Ka with tiny pieces of his, but he couldn't be persuaded to say any more. Hawkins didn't need persuading!

He said, 'Topher, have I ever told you of the Battle of San Juan?'

He had – it had happened years before, but there was no stopping him. 'It was in 1567 . . .'

As he spoke, in his rolling Devonshire burr, he stuffed a clay pipe with tobacco, the spicy substance he'd brought back from the New Found Lands, and as he described how a Spanish cannon had once blown a cup of beer right out of his hand, but thrown him backwards so that he lived to fight another day, smoke spiralled up to the ceiling, which was patterned with a lattice of roses.

'So what do you think I did, Master Dee?' he said suddenly. 'What do you think I said to my men?'

'Fear not!' said Frobisher, who obviously knew the story too. *For God, who hath preserved me from this shot will also deliver us from these traitors and villains!* Then he said, 'I only hope the Almighty is looking after your kinsman as well as he looked after you.'

Then they were all silent, for Hawkins' young kinsman was Francis Drake who had set off the previous December, to sail westwards right round the world. But now it was summer and there had been no news of him for months.

Jane said, 'I am supposed to be entertaining Master Dee, filling him with good cheer. I had orders from the Queen.'

Frobisher said, ''E'll have good cheer if what I 'ear of the Queen's plans for you is true.'

'May shall marry September twice if Her Majesty has her way,' said Hawkins.

What were they talking about? Why did everyone speak in riddles?

Shortly afterwards the two men left, asking Topher to carry greetings to his father and when they'd gone Jane said, 'They think highly of Dr Dee and . . . so do I. He is a very great man.'

And looking up from stroking Ka, Topher noticed that

her cheeks were red.

'I think,' said Jane, but didn't finish, as his father came into the room and Topher saw how much she liked him and how he liked her. So he was not completely surprised when his father announced – on the way home – that he and Jane wished to marry. Fortunately, the Queen approved.

Goody Faldo didn't approve. According to her, the Queen had match-maked the whole thing. May marrying September must be the latest fashion, she said, for the Queen at the age of forty-five was planning to marry the French Duc d'Anjou who was only twenty-three! Goody – like everyone else in England she said – was against it.

Topher learned all this later that evening when she was giving him his supper, after Doctor Dee had returned to Richemount to eat. Goody also said she'd heard that Jane Fromond was waspish, and that was why she was still unwed at the age of twenty-two. Nobody else would have her.

Topher didn't say anything. He hadn't found Jane at all waspish, but he didn't want to disagree with Goody, in case she took umbrage and stopped talking. He loved hearing her gossip. It was the way he found out things. So he supped his barley beer and ate the oatcakes she'd made, and it soon became clear that the old woman was worried. The new young mistress might decide she didn't need her as housekeeper, then where would she be – on the streets like the beggars? As he clambered into bed that night and pulled the curtains round, Topher wondered how his life would change. Stepmothers were common enough. Many of his school friends had step-mothers, but his father had been a long time unwed.

The wedding, a few months later, was a quiet affair in the parish church, but the celebration – the Queen's gift to two people she liked very much, was a grand affair at Richemount Palace. It began at noon and carried on till late at night. Afterwards Topher could only remember moments of it, most vividly the candle-lit Masque in the Great Hall in which the Queen took the part of Hymen, goddess of Marriage. She sang a song in praise of love and her singing voice was sweet, much sweeter than her speaking voice, and she did look very beautiful singing and playing the lute, robed in white and garlanded with flowers, and the Duc d'Anjou whom nobody liked, obviously thought so too. Later, Topher, watching from the minstrels' gallery, remembered him dancing the volta with her, lifting her so high off the ground that everyone saw her gold-lace stockings!

But soon after that he, Topher, must have fallen asleep for when he woke up he was back in Mortlake, chilly in his four-poster bed and Goody Faldo was shouting at him to get up and go to school! For Goody needn't have worried about the marriage. Doctor Dee insisted that she stay and enjoy her old age in his house, though Jane would take over most of her duties.

But getting Topher up was one duty she retained!

'Come *on*, Master Dee!' she scolded him, but it was February and there was ice on the windowpanes. 'Come *on*! If you are late the schoolmaster will beat you.'

He did move then for Goody was right. He'd be beaten if he was late. He'd be beaten if he forgot his hornbook or if he failed his daily Latin test. So mumbling his conjugations, he pulled on his clothes. '*Amo, amas, amat, ama . . .*' What on earth came next? He tried to remember as he ate his breakfast of bread and cheese.

'Mwa!' Ka was no help – she just wanted to share his cheese.

Jane *was* a help. He needn't have worried about the marriage either. It was better having a mother again, especially such a clever one. She helped him learn his lessons, and though she wasn't patient she tried to be. She was fiery, she said, she couldn't help it. But Doctor Dee liked his fiery wife – that was obvious. He laughed a lot more, and Topher saw him more often, though he still spent most of his time in his workrooms with his books and instruments. Yes, life did seem much better. It was a Saturday when matters took a turn for the worse, though in the morning it looked as if it was going to be a really jolly day.

Topher was delighted when Jane told him they were going to see a play. He'd seen plays before, of course, in the market place at Whitsuntide when the trade guilds rolled in their wagons and acted out scenes from the Bible, and in the tavern yard sometimes when travelling players came to the village. But this play was being put on in the Theatre, a new building built especially for putting on plays all the year round because people liked them so much. James Burbage, the leader of the Earl of Leicester's players who sometimes performed at court, had had it built, east of the City, in Shoreditch – and everybody was talking about it.

They set off before noon in the doctor's river-boat, and though the river was busy, because lots of other people had the same idea, they made good speed. There was a lively west wind and the familiar landmarks soon appeared – the Abbey of West Minster, Whitehall Palace, and once they'd rounded the bend in the river, the City itself with the spire of St Paul's church against the skyline. But it wasn't till they had passed under London Bridge that they got their first glimpse of the Theatre and then they couldn't be sure they were really seeing it. It was about a mile away.

'There it is!' said Jane as they pulled into Lyone's Key, pointing to a pennant, fluttering high from a turret topping a circular thatch.

'Are you sure?' said the doctor.

'Yes, it's got the rose on it, look!'

Jane was right, they saw when they got nearer, though the bull ring and the bear garden nearby also had the rose-flag flying above them and a trumpeter trumpeting a fanfare.

Tantara! Tantara! Tatta-tatta-tantara! It was as if the three trumpeters were competing!

But the fanfare from the Theatre was loudest, Topher thought, as he tried to keep close to his father and Jane, as they made their way through the crowds! You could hear it, over the cries of the street sellers, over the barks of the baiting dogs, over the shouts of the crowds pushing and shoving to get to their Saturday entertainment.

Taran-tata! Taran-tata!

Jane urged haste as the doctor stopped to take a pamphlet from a man selling them, near the entrance, for the play was due to start, she said. Fortunately they were nearly there. In fact they were nearer than they thought, at the end of a line of people queuing to pay and enter by a narrow doorway. The queue seemed to move slowly, but at last the doctor was paying – for superior seats in the upper gallery – and they were climbing a dark stair-case to reach them. Then they were in daylight again, at their seats, looking down on the stage – where several fashionable young men were sitting – as if they thought everyone had come to see them, not the play. Below them, the circular yard was packed with standing spec-tators, some quaffing beer or cracking nuts, all of them talking loudly. In the galleries people called to each other from one side of the yard to the other. From the cockpit nearby a cock crowed.

Then the trumpeter played a very loud fanfare and announced that the play was going to begin, and an actor stepped onto the stage. It was young Will Shakespeare, someone said, a very talented young man. Someone else said they thought he'd written the play – it was by a Mr S – and he'd be taking the part of Tib the maid later. But gradually, most of the crowd quietened down, and the actor began,

'As Gammer Gurton with many a wide stitch
Sat piecing and patching of Hodge her man's britch,
By chance or misfortune, as she her gear tost,
In Hodge' leather breeches her needle she lost . . .'

The play was called *Gammer Gurton's Needle* and that is what it was about, a lost needle. It was very silly and a bit unseemly. Topher and Jane laughed a lot but Doctor Dee didn't. He kept looking at the pamphlet he'd been handed as he came in. Topher had caught a glimpse of it:

Discovery of a Gaping Gulf Wherein England is like to be swallowed by Another French Marriage . . .

He guessed it must be about the Queen and the Duc d'Anjou, and wasn't altogether surprised when, at the end of the first act, his father said he must go. He didn't say where, but did say he'd take a skiff as it was faster and leave his boat for Jane and Topher to return to Mortlake.

When Jane and Topher reached the boat in the early evening after the play had ended, Jane said the skiff obviously hadn't been fast enough, for a street crier was telling a highly interested crowd that the writer of the seditious pamphlet, a man called John Stubbs, had been arrested and punished. His right hand had been cut off. Seditious? Had the pamphlet been seditious? Had it really threatened the Queen? There was even worse news than that. A wax image of the Queen with pins in it had been found at Lincoln's Inn Fields. Its maker was being sought and he or she would be severely punished.

When they reached home Doctor Dee wasn't there. Nor was Ka. Goody Faldo said she'd always said the cat would get the good doctor in trouble. They'd probably been arrested for sorcery. She wouldn't be surprised if the two of them were in the Tower.

Chapter 14

Goody said the mark of the heathen on the cat didn't help. She meant the key sign on Ka's forehead, the sign of life to the Ancient Egyptians. Heathens that they were, said Goody, they worshipped cats, and some people gave the impression that they did. Ignoring Jane's warning looks she went on, 'Cats should sleep in barns not bedchambers.'

Ka often slept on Topher's bed.

'Shut up, Goody.' Now Jane *was* waspish. 'Doctor Dee has *not* been arrested. He is *not* in danger. There is no one the Queen values more highly. These are troubled times and he has gone to advise her.'

Goody said that keeping a cat just gave fuel to the doctor's enemies. Then she left the room muttering about only trying to help.

Topher said, 'What enemies? Who are my father's enemies? I thought my father was in good favour with Queen Elizabeth.'

Jane said he was, but there were those who were jealous of this, who said he was a magician and accused him of practising alchemy.

'What's alchemy?'

It was the search for the Philosopher's Stone, she said, the substance which would turn base metal into gold.

'What's wrong with that?' He knew – his father had

told him – that all substances were composed of one primitive matter, the *prima materia*, which was forged into different forms by different processes. What was wrong with trying to change one material into another?

'It's a punishable offence. It's against the law,' said Jane.

'Why?'

She didn't answer.

'*Does* he do it?'

She didn't answer that either, just said that they must eat, and then he must go to bed. And he had the feeling that she was just as worried as Goody was, which made him feel worried too. He remembered what the Queen had called his father – my map-making magician – and how he'd only half-denied it. 'My magic is of Mathematics and Measurements, Your Majesty.' That's what he'd said.

Was he a magician? Was he an alchemist? Was he a Welsh wizard?

When Goody didn't bring their supper, Jane went to the kitchen to arrange it, looking as if she was going to sting someone, and Topher went into the garden. Ka liked being out at twilight; there were lots of moths flitting about it. He liked it too; the scent of lavender and stock drowned some of the less pleasant smells – from the stinking jakes at the end of the garden for instance.

Well, he wouldn't find Ka there! He hoped he'd find her rolling around somewhere, tipsy on the silver mint she loved so much, or watching for voles on the river-bank, but she wasn't in either place and the river was quiet. There wasn't even a rowing boat in sight. Everything was quiet. It was as if everyone was staying inside, lying low, keeping out of trouble.

He went inside, to search the house again, but there was no sign of her. She especially liked to sleep on newly-washed linen, so he went upstairs and looked in the linen chest on the landing – just in case she'd jumped in while a serving-maid was getting something out, but there was nothing, not a tell-tale hair or pawmark.

So he went out again, to the work rooms his father had had built in the garden, to house all his books and instruments. Some people said he had the biggest library in England. He'd rescued lots of books from the monasteries which had been destroyed by King Henry. There were lots of books in all the rooms, and in some lots of bottles of different shapes and sizes with liquids bubbling in them. In others strange-looking instruments stood on tables or hung from beams – compasses and astrolabes and the telescope that Captain Drake called the Bring 'em Near! And the cross staff for measuring shadows and working out latitudes and the back staff which was even better. His father certainly did a lot of measuring and a lot of looking at things. He spent hours studying the stars and making changes to the maps and charts which hung on the walls or covered tables. Or he changed them when travellers returned with information about new lands or new seas.

New lands! New seas! New foods! New instruments! For a while he felt sympathy for Goody Faldo – no wonder she felt that her poor old head was spinning – but then he remembered what she'd said about his father and sorcery. Was his father a sorcerer? Were his books about magic? What was inside them? He scanned their titles – *Ephemeris Anno 1557* by John Field, *De Revolutionibus Orbium Celestium* by Copernicus, and *The Key of Solomon*. He lifted that one down – and it *was* about magic! It contained spells for finding lost objects including treasure! You could use a key and a pendulum or a piece of paper and a key – or mirrors! Is that how his father found things?

After supper, when he went upstairs to bed, he opened the door of the mirror room. Often at night he'd pulled back his bed curtains and seen – under the door which didn't fit too well – lights flashing on on off. In patterns, he was sure of that. Codes. Stepping inside the room, he glanced out of the window and thought he could see the lights of the Palace of Richemount.

Was his father there with the Queen now? Or was he in one of her other palaces? Was Ka with him? Was Jane really not worried as she'd said to Goody? She hadn't eaten much supper, though the sparrow stew with sippets of toasted bread smelled delicious – of cloves and rosemary as well as meat. Nor had he eaten much. Twice she'd said, 'I'm sure your father is being a great comfort to Her Majesty. She'll be much troubled by this image business.'

Image business – the wax model of the Queen stuck with pins – it spoke of witchcraft and witchhunts. When they happened it was bad news for everyone. Queen Mary had accused his father of making an image of her. It was bad news for cats and people who owned them.

Before he climbed into bed he prayed for the Queen, he prayed for his father and Jane, he prayed to God to save his soul as he always did, and he prayed that Ka wasn't being pursued by the mob.

Chapter 15

He woke up hearing church bells, pulled back the bed curtains and shot out of bed! Seven already! School began at seven! Why hadn't Goody woken him? Then, looking out of the window, he saw Francis Hutchinson, their neighbour, coming out of his front door, followed by his wife and six children all dressed in sober black and white – and he breathed again. It was Sunday! Bliss! They were on their way to church. He saw them stop at the end of the street as a rowdy gang of boys came into it, kicking a ball. Then he heard Francis ranting about sin and the Sabbath – he was well known for his Puritanical views – but seconds later Wat, the miller's boy, passed beneath Topher's window, still kicking the ball – and he just missed getting the contents of Mistress Pottle's pisspot on his head.

As she went inside the street went quiet except for a line of ducks quacking their way to the river and a skinny dog peeing against Mistress Pottle's wall. It wasn't till he saw a rat running up the central ditch that he remembered Ka. Ka! How could he forget her? Bliss shattered, he recalled the happenings of the day before.

She wasn't on his bed – he checked that first. Where was she? Where was his father?

Pulling off his nightshirt and pulling on his stockings, he listened as he planned where to look next. Someone was about, probably the servants, but it was Jane who met him at the bottom of the stairs a few minutes later, her cloak round her shoulders. She was going to Richemount, she said. Ka hadn't returned and neither had his father, but she had had a message from him. He had stayed the night at the palace.

Topher asked if he could go with her. She said yes if he put on his ruff. They might see the Queen and disorderly dress was disrespectful. When he came down again, she gave him an apple to eat on the way. Then they set off – on foot – because it was quicker than waiting for the horse to be harnessed.

As always the walk across the park was peaceful, but the atmosphere at Richemount was very different from the last time he'd come. Even before they got to the palace, guards bristling with pikes and muskets stopped them. There were guards at all the approach roads to the palace, stopping people and searching them.

Jane accepted this – patiently for her – but she was less patient when the guards at the palace gate wouldn't let her straight in. She said she was Mistress Dee, wife of Her Majesty's adviser Doctor Dee and a member of the royal household herself till recently. She told them they recognised her – and some of them did, but not the reinforcements who had been brought in, and no one was taking any chances. An insurrection was feared. You could feel the fear and the suspicion. They asked her to name someone inside who would come and identify her. Then they had to wait for Lady Howard, to whom Jane had once been lady-in-waiting.

As they waited Topher scanned the landscape for sight of Ka. If there were any cats around they had the sense to stay out of sight.

The low grey clouds added to the atmosphere of oppression. It was a summer's day, but it felt cold. The flags above the palace drooped.

It seemed ages before Lady Howard appeared, but at last she did, a large lady, looking like a galleon in full sail as she moved over the blue-green flowerbeds towards them – and sounding like a town crier. She greeted Jane crossly, having not forgiven her for leaving her service, she said, and did not like being summoned like a serving wench.

As he followed the two women to the palace entrance Topher kept a lookout for Ka, and heard without any earstrain that the Queen was greatly agitated; that Lady Howard had never seen her so agitated, that she was vexed about the opposition to her proposed marriage and she feared a Spanish invasion, that she feared a civil war after her death if not before it and she was worried about Mary Queen of Scots. In short the matter of the waxen image had upset her deeply. The whole court had been surprised how much it had upset her, for she had lived with plots against her all her life. But all her old health problems of toothache and leg pains had returned.

'And she connects the pains with the pins, of course.' Lady Howard sounded as if she connected it too, but Doctor Dee, it seemed, didn't. He had been hours with the Queen telling her such enchantments were not possible, and he was still with her. She would not let him go.

'He tells her it is folly to believe it, for it is the believing that gives the pain!' said Lady Howard.

'Yes,' Jane nodded and Lady Howard looked surprised.

'Well, he should know,' she said shortly.

'What do you mean?' said Jane, but her former mistress didn't reply. They were at the front entrance and the panelled entrance hall buzzed with the talk of important-looking people. Topher recognised Lord Burghley, the Queen's Secretary of State and Sir Thomas Bromley, the Lord Chancellor, but he couldn't see his father.

Smoke curled up to the ceiling as a tobacco pipe was passed from one man to another. Feet tapped impatiently. One man strode up and down the hall.

Most stared as Lady Howard sailed past them all, stopping for just a few moments to speak with her own husband, followed by Jane and Topher. They would wait in the elephant room, she said to Jane. The Queen and Doctor Dee were in her private chamber on the other side of the entrance hall. The Privy Council, which included her husband, were being made to wait outside. They dare not leave in case she called for one of them.

Jane didn't say anything, which was probably wise. Lady Howard was obviously not pleased that her former lady-in-waiting's husband was taking precedence over hers.

When Jane was seated Lady Howard said she needed to speak to her husband. She opened the door and Topher saw Ka!

It was a fleeting glimpse – as she raced towards the staircase – but certain it was her, he dashed out, turned sharply right and saw her again, disappearing round a curve in the staircase. Was she heading for the gallery

where he'd found her before beneath the throne? He set off after her – swiftly, silently and, he hoped, unseen by the men in the hall. Something told him that it would not do to be seen chasing a cat. Old beliefs still held sway in at least some of the old men's heads. Few were as learned as his father. Some still thought that the earth was the centre of the universe, though Copernicus had proved otherwise nearly fifty years ago. So, keeping close to the bannisters and trying not to slip on the polished wood, he followed her and was pleased to hear no change in the hum of conversation below him. Ka too must have got by them without being seen.

Unfortunately when he reached the small landing at the top, he couldn't see her either. On his right were the double doors to the throne room, but the doors didn't open as they had on his first visit. There was no one there to open them – on the outside anyway. He pushed them. They stayed shut. Then how had Ka got in? She must have got in because she wasn't there.

Standing on tiptoe he peered through the keyhole – and there at the end of the long empty room was the canopied throne on a dais, with no one on it. Of course not. The Queen was downstairs with his father. No Ka either. Of course no Ka. She certainly couldn't have opened the door. Then where had she gone? She hadn't gone downstairs again. He would have seen her.

Examining the narrow landing more carefully, he saw that it was no more than a small passage really. In fact, as he took a few more steps he realised it *was* a small passage, with a door at the end of it, an open door, hidden in the dark oak panelling. That must be why he hadn't noticed it before! The dark oak panelling concealed the dark entrance to a closet very effectively, would have concealed it completely when the door was closed.

'Ka.' Peering in, he whispered her name, then made soft sucking noises with his mouth, because she sometimes responded to that, expecting to see her amber eyes shining out of the darkness. She was probably scared, if she'd been chased or had things thrown at her. That could well have happened. She'd looked as if she was fleeing from something when he'd first seen her. She could even have been shot at. He remembered the soldiers' muskets.

'Ka, it's me.' Crouching, he felt inside – and felt nothing.

He reached further in – and still felt nothing. It was a very deep closet. He stepped inside it with his hands stretched out before him, took another step and another and another – and still he didn't come to a wall – and with a jolt he realised it wasn't a closet. He was in another passage!

What now? He stepped back. It was dark and he wasn't fond of the dark. He ought to go back to Jane. It wasn't wise to go exploring in the residence of the Queen of England. Especially at a time when she suspected everything that moved.

But what about Ka? He called her again, raising his voice slightly. 'Ka! Ka!' Then he made the soft sucking noises again, willing her to come to him.

Where did this passage lead? He tried hard to get his bearings and worked out that he must be standing over the entrance hall where the Privy Council was waiting. He listened. Yes. He thought he could hear the murmur of their voices below. The passage led off to his right. Surely Ka would come out of it in her own good time? If he went down now, leaving the door open she would be sure to come out.

But then worrying thoughts came into his head. What if someone saw her who wasn't kindly disposed towards her? What if someone came along and closed the door? What if it were a dead end? She'd be trapped.

He stepped forward again and as his eyes got used to the darkness he found he could see better. Or was there light coming in from the other end? The passage seemed to be a gap between two expanses of wood panelling, between two rooms. He moved along it quite quickly and the voices below got fainter and fainter, till he couldn't hear them any more, even when he stopped and listened hard. Then, as he advanced and the passage narrowed, other voices took their place, voices he recognised! They were very clear, were coming up a chimney stack. That was what was narrowing his path. The Queen's shrill whisper voice floated up the chimney.

'You *must* find it.'

What was she talking about?

'It will be the answer to all our problems – England's problems.'

His father – for surely she must be speaking to his father? – didn't answer.

'We will be able to refurbish the Navy.'

Doctor Dee spoke now. 'There is no need just yet. My investigations tell me that there will be no Spanish Invasion till 1588. And Francis Drake will return to rout the Spanish Armada, Your Majesty.'

It was 1580, the twenty-second year of her reign.

"'Tis well to be prepared,' she replied. '*Find it.*'

What did she mean? What was this 'it'?

'Find it and we shall be truly *riche* in Richemount!' She laughed at her own wit. 'Find them both and there will be no more worries about the succession!'

'Your Majesty, I cannot promise to find them.' His father sounded tired.

'You can promise to *try*.'

'I am mindful that the last of your advisers to *try* ended his days in the Tower, Your Majesty.'

'Ah, poor stupid Cornelius, he failed,' sighed the Queen. 'You are cleverer, Doctor Dee. You will find the Stone *and* the Elixir.'

Did she mean the Philosopher's Stone? But Jane said that was a punishable offence. It was against the law. So why was the Queen asking his father to find it and what was the Elixir?

Below, there was a sound of moving chairs. The meeting it seemed was at a close.

And he felt something brushing against his legs. A rat? For a moment he froze, then he heard a purr! Ka! He picked her up, felt sticky, spiky trembling fur. What on earth had happened to her? Was she injured? Desperate to examine her, he began to make his way along the passage. But before he reached the door he'd left open, he came to a dead end.

Chapter 16

Where was the door? It was completely dark. He couldn't see anything, even if there were anything to see. From the outside the door had looked like all the other wooden panels. It hadn't got a handle. It probably looked the same from the inside too.

'Sorry Ka, I've got to put you down and use my hands.'

She kept close to him as he moved along, probing the wall with his fingers. It was comforting to feel her nudging his legs. He hoped the stickiness he'd felt on her fur wasn't blood. He wondered about shouting for help, but decided it was too risky. He'd rather no one knew that he'd been in a position to spy on the Queen. Not that he had been spying, not deliberately, but that's how it would look. There was such a lot to think about – the Queen's command to his father for instance – *Find it!* – but he'd think about that later when he was out of here. Who or what had closed the door? Had someone deliberately trapped him? Forcing himself to keep calm, he started to feel the wall on his left again. The dead-end wall extended high above him – that posed another problem. What if the opening mechanism was high up? Or what if it were on the right-hand wall?

He must have felt every square inch of the passage before he sat down to reconsider his position. How long had he been gone? Who knew he was missing? Had he told Jane he was going after Ka? Wouldn't she be wondering by now? Would Lady Howard have asked where he'd gone? One thought cheered him up: by now his father might know – and he was good at finding things! That was another reason people consulted him – to find mislaid objects and missing persons. Topher remembered the books of magic he'd found, and the Queen had referred to his Magical Rods.

'He's so clever, Ka. I'm sure he'll find us.'

She was in the v of his lap – his knees were nearly under his chin – purring a snuffly purr. The doctor had found treasure once, in a field, buried beneath the ground. He'd found water too, where no water seemed to be. Mistress Cotton had called him because her well had dried up. He'd walked round her garden holding his Magical Rods and suddenly they'd started to jiggle in his hands. Her manservant started digging and suddenly there was a spring of water! He'd found her a place for a new well!

'He'll find us, Ka. The famous Doctor Dee will find us. I just hope he won't take too long.'

Topher was hungry and felt a bit sick. All he'd had for breakfast was an apple. It must be time for the midday meal. Ka purred, slightly less snuffly now.

Don't wo . . . rrry. Don't wo . . . rrry. He'll come. He'll come.

It was Ka who heard him first. Topher felt her hearing him; he felt her claws in his thigh as she stiffened slightly. But she didn't grip. She wasn't afraid. And suddenly it was lighter, and there was his father's white beard and

107

piercing blue eyes peering at them through the opening.

They didn't need telling to come out, and the doctor, who was alone, didn't tell them to. He just stood back and let them pass and closed the panel behind them. Then, as he was brushing the dust from Topher's breeches, he said, 'You were looking for the kitchens? You were looking for something to eat, child?'

He seemed to be telling rather than asking, and before they rounded the curve in the staircase he took Ka from Topher and slipped her between the folds of his black gown, into one of his many pockets, Topher assumed. She made no objection. When they reached the bottom of the stairs, Jane came out of the elephant room. The Privy Council must have been called in by Her Majesty, because the entrance hall was empty, except for the soldiers at the door.

They took a boat home. Fortunately they didn't have to wait for the right tide this far up the river, and it wasn't long before a boatman responded to his father's cry of 'Oars!'

Ka stayed in the doctor's pocket during the half-hour voyage. She stayed out of sight till they were safely inside their house in Mortlake, eating a meal of rabbit pie and stuffed pike. The doctor didn't eat much, Topher noticed, and he looked very tired and worried. He had slept very little the previous night, he said. Her Majesty had needed a great deal of reassurance, but he had convinced her that the wax image was simply part of a plot to undermine her confidence. He had advised that she see it only as a measure of public opinion regarding certain aspects of her policies. This vexed her, he said.

She knew immediately that he meant her proposed marriage, but he had managed to calm her. He said all this to Jane as the two of them sat at table. They both seemed to forget Topher, standing at the other end, feeding Ka with choice morsels. She liked the rabbit pie but didn't think much of the pike flavoured with orange and ginger. As she ate, he was able to examine her. Poor Ka! She looked as if she'd had all sorts of stuff thrown at her – and the skin under her neck was raw.

'The Queen wants a child,' he heard his father say. 'That is her motivation, to solve the problem of the succession.'

'She is forty-five,' said Jane, who was big with child herself. 'It's unlikely that she will have one, however young her husband, and people do not wish her to marry at all. They certainly don't want her to marry a Frenchman. They believed her when she said she was wedded to them, to England.'

After Ka had eaten she went and sat in the window seat overlooking the back garden. Then she started to wash herself. When he had permission Topher went and sat with her, and his father joined them. He said he would make some ointment for Ka's sore neck.

Later, when his father had applied the ointment he went upstairs. He needed to rest, he said. Topher joined Jane who was sitting in the garden. She was smocking a robe for the baby she was going to have, but she asked him if he would like her to play the lute or play chequers with him, or listen to his lessons. And though he would have preferred a game of chequers, he said he would like her to listen to his lesson, because there was a new Latin

109

declension he was going to be tested on. If he didn't know it he would be whipped. Then he remembered that he'd left his primer by his bed, so he went upstairs to get it and met his father on the landing, outside the mirror room. After hesitating for a moment, he said, 'Topher, I am going to need your help.' And drawing Topher into the room, he said, 'You heard the Queen. I know you did. You know that she wants me to find the Philosopher's Stone?'

'Yes, Father.'

'Well, I must find it, you know that?'

'Yes, Father.'

'The Queen will be obeyed,' the doctor went on. 'And I have been trying for many a long year.'

But it was against the law. It was sorcery!

'It isn't sorcery, Topher.'

Could his father read his thoughts?

'I do not, have not practised the black arts, and I will not, but all my experiments so far have come to nothing. I have tried Mechanical Magic and Mathematical Magic, Natural Magic and Divine Magic. I have asked the angels themselves for help, but they have not answered me. It is because I am old, Topher. They would speak to you.'

What did his father mean? Topher was confused and afraid. Jane's words came back to him. Seeking the Philosopher's Stone was a punishable offence. It was sorcery! His father's enemies said he was a sorcerer – and he was!

'It isn't sorcery, Topher. I ask the *angels*. Angels are the Lord God's messengers, not Beelzebub's, and angels speak to young innocent children. Boys, or maids of ten or eleven years make the best scryers. Trimethius himself

110

says so.'

Scryers? What were they?

Scrying was reading, the doctor explained, and for a moment Topher thought he might be able to help but then the doctor said it was the reading of *crystals* and *mirrors*.

He drew Topher towards a globe on a covered table near the window, not a spherical map of the world, but a sphere of pink glass which shone in the evening sun. It was beautiful.

'What can you see, Topher?'

'I – I can see a beautiful pink glass.'

'What else?'

'I can see lights shining in it, lights like sparks.' They flashed and sparkled, seemed to leap out of the gleaming sphere as the evening sun shone through the window.

'And . . .' his father prompted.

'I can see the pattern of the tapestry beneath.' The tapestry's rich jewel colours were reflected in the base of the sphere.

'And . . .'

'I can see my own reflection.' He couldn't help smiling to see his own face glowing rosy pink!

But his father seemed disappointed. 'You are tired. I am tired. We shall try again tomorrow, for we shall succeed. We shall succeed. We will not disappoint Her Majesty. You can go now, Topher.'

Then he laid his hand on Topher's shoulder. 'Just one other thing. Do not tell Jane. It would worry her and she should not be worried when she is so near her time. Do not tell anyone. It is our secret, yes?'

Topher went downstairs forgetting all about his Latin

111

primer. He had the feeling that there was an even greater test ahead and failing it would result in worse than a beating.

Chapter 17

He told Ka about it that night, whispering under the heavy covers, the bed curtains tightly closed.

'What shall I do, Ka?'

She lay in the cave he'd made, in darkness so complete he couldn't see her, but he could hear her purring, could feel her fur against his skin.

Jane had said that seeking the Philosopher's Stone was a punishable offence, but his father had said that someone called Cornelius – poor stupid Cornelius the Queen had called him – ended his days in the Tower because he *hadn't* found it. He didn't want his father to end his days in the Tower. He knew what that meant.

But seeking the Philosopher's Stone was alchemy and alchemy was against the law. Jane had said so. But didn't the Queen make the law? Or did Parliament?

Even with Ka's comforting presence he found it hard to get to sleep, and when he did, it seemed no time at all before Goody Faldo was shaking his shoulder, waking him up for school.

'It's six of the clock, young Master.'

As he raced to put on his clothes, he tried to focus on the day ahead, for it would not do to forget anything. Downstairs he checked that his quill pen and ink horn, knife and primer were inside his satchel, and as he ate the bread Goody insisted on, he went over his Latin.

'*Mensa, mensa, mens* . . .

'Don't talk with your mouth full, young Master!'

He said the rest under his breath.

Later, he wished he'd eaten more, for when he came home from school at midday his father was waiting for him – Jane had gone to visit her sister he said – and there was no meal on the table. It would better effect the *scrying*, he said, if they fasted beforehand, and when Topher came home from afternoon school, his father led him straight to the mirror room, where the crystal globe stood on a table, but today it looked like an altar. Overlaid with a white cloth, there were candles on either side of it. Nearby was a ewer of water and a bowl. Solemnly Doctor Dee poured some water and washed and dried his hands.

Then, telling Topher to kneel, he washed and dried Topher's hands. Then he got down on his knees.

'Father, Son and Holy Ghost, Three in One, Holy Trinity, Assist us in this work and send us thy Messengers.'

Out of the corner of his eye, which he knew should have been tightly shut, Topher saw Ka slide into the room. He closed his eyes and she settled beside him. He could hear her purring in the silence. The doctor must have heard her too but he didn't object. After what seemed an age he said, 'Open your eyes, child.' Topher opened his eyes.

'Look only at the crystal, child.'

He gazed at it.

The weather today was overcast and there was no evening sun streaming through the window.

'What can you see, child?'

'The beautiful pink glass, Father.' There were no lights leaping from it today.

'What else?'

'A glow in its centre, Father.' There was a dim glow.

'Watch that glowing centre, child.'

He watched but his knees hurt. He could feel the wooden floorboards pressing into them, even through the thick cloth of his breeches, but he still tried hard to concentrate on the golden glow in the centre of the sphere. And after a while it seemed to flicker and so did something in his head, so that he couldn't take his eyes off the shining centre which grew bigger and smaller like a flame.

'What can you see now, child?'

'The glowing, . . . er, flickering centre, Father.' His own voice seemed to come from afar, not from his own head which seemed fuzzy and blurred. Now he couldn't feel his painful knees, couldn't feel any other part of his body. There was just his eyes and the crystal before him which seemed to be fading or misting up.

'Tell me exactly what you see, child.'

Topher told him about the mist in the glass and thought he detected some excitement in his father's voice as he said, 'I shall summon the angels now, boy.'

Then, his father started to chant. 'One times nine is nine. Two times nine is eighteen . . .'

Later, Topher thought he remembered him saying, 'Nine times nine . . .' but he couldn't remember any more, because soon after he fainted. He did remember coming round though. His head was between his knees and his father was holding a small bottle to his nostrils.

The strong smell made him sneeze.

'Bless you, child.' His father spoke kindly and was apologetic.

He said Topher had done very well but he must have gone too long without food. That was his – the doctor's – fault; he should have chosen a better time. Sunday would be better, when Topher didn't have to go to school, and Sunday was a holy day. They would try again on Sunday as soon as they had risen. Then he wouldn't have to go all day without food. That was nearly a week away. In the meantime, said the doctor, he would teach Topher some of what he knew, so that he would understand what they were doing.

For the rest of the week, in the evening, after school, they went into one of his father's book-lined rooms and he showed Topher what he called mathematical tables. There were hundreds of them. He was showing Topher the simplest, he said, and he most wanted him to understand the Nine Times Table and the Mystical Concept of Nine. The science of alchemy was in the ninth house of the zodiac, he said.

'Nine is a magical number, the Triple Triad, three times three, which is a divine number. Look at the Nine Times Table, child.' He wrote it on a wax tablet.

$1 \times 9 = 9$
$2 \times 9 = 18$
$3 \times 9 = 27$

The $\times$ sign stood for the words 'multiplied by', he said, and the $=$ sign meant 'equals'. The doctor himself had devised these signs to make mathematics easier. There was also + for 'add' and − for 'subtract' and ÷ for 'divide', but today they were *multiplying*.

At first Topher found it confusing, so the doctor made rows and rows of nines on a counting frame, to show how the numbers grew. Then he got Topher to count them. It took ages. Then he showed how the tables could do the counting for him *quickly*, but it was when the doctor showed him the whole table, and said, 'Add the second two digits together!' that he began to realise the power of number nine.

$1 \times 9 = 9$ .... $9 + 0 = 9$
$2 \times 9 = 18$ .... $1 + 8 = 9$
$3 \times 9 = 27$ .... $2 + 7 = 9$
$4 \times 9 = 36$ .... $3 + 6 = 9$
$5 \times 9 = 45$ .... $4 + 5 = 9$
$6 \times 9 = 54$ .... $5 + 4 = 9$
$7 \times 9 = 63$ .... $6 + 3 = 9$
$8 \times 9 = 72$ .... $7 + 2 = 9$
$9 \times 9 = 81$ .... $8 + 1 = 9$

However many times you did it, you always came back to nine! He multiplied 187×9 and the same thing happened! Nine wouldn't go away! But could it, would it bring angels down from Heaven above?

Why were they summoning angels? He asked his father.

'To tell us the secret, of course, of the Philosopher's Stone and the Elixir. How could you forget, boy?' His father lifted down one of his heavy tomes. 'And it can be good, Topher. Look what Lyly says.' Opening the book he began to read,

Philosopher's Stone.
It is a blessing beyond all blessings upon earth, given to
but very few, and to those few rather by revelation of the
good angels of God than the proper industry of man.

Nevertheless, Goody Faldo wasn't impressed. Coming to
the door, one night, to tell them that supper was ready,
she saw what they were doing and muttered that it
looked like wizardry. It didn't help that Ka was in the
room with them. She loved watching her reflection in
the crystal.

'That's why she has nine lives, is it?'

'It could be so,' said the doctor, who always answered
questions when he could. He believed in conquering
ignorance with knowledge, he said. So when Topher
asked what he'd been meaning to ask for sometime,
'What is the Elixir, father?' – the doctor paused only to
check that the door was closed, before he said, 'Why, it
is the Secret of Eternal Life, child. The Queen wants me
to find it so that she will live for ever.'

And you have to find it if you don't want to end up
like poor Cornelius, thought Topher. He longed to help
his father.

But on Sunday when they tried again it didn't work.
Topher concentrated as hard as he could on the glass in
front of him, while his father prayed and chanted the
table, but no angels appeared. Nine times they tried – it
took them all day. His father asked the angels to make
themselves known, to speak even if they didn't show
themselves, but they didn't speak. Topher saw the light

at the centre of the crystal but nothing else, nothing else at all. And at last the doctor said that Topher could eat and go to bed, and as he climbed the stairs with Ka in his arms, he heard a knocking on the street door. Glancing back as Robert, the serving man, opened it, he saw a man with his hat so low it covered half his face – and Ka stiffened.

Chapter 18

The man said he was Edward Talbot, a ship's victualler from Deptford, here to do business with Doctor Dee, but he wasn't. He'd said that just to get past Robert, and as he entered the living room Jane gasped, 'Ned Kelley!'

When he took his hat off, even Topher recognised him, despite his black hair which was long like a peasant's, because he had no ears, and his bony earless face had appeared on billboards round the town. The man in the room below was the notorious Ned Kelley who had been tried by the Star Chamber and found guilty – of forging coins. That's why his ears had been cut off! Jane, sitting in the inglenook, looked to her husband to repel the impostor, but Doctor Dee was not unwelcoming. The man said, straightaway, that he was Ned Kelley – there was no point in denying it after all – but he also said he'd been wrongly convicted, and Doctor Dee stood listening to him. *Why*? And why did he take up with him?

Jane and Topher often discussed it afterwards.

Was it Kelley's silver tongue? Certainly, that night he told such a tale – of intrigue and mistaken identity and wrongful arrest – with a skill worthy of one of the Earl of Leicester's players. But Jane didn't believe him. Topher didn't believe him – and surely, surely the doctor didn't

121

believe him? He knew everyone in the Star Chamber!

So why did he invite him to stay? For that's what he did – that very night, to Jane's expressed displeasure. It was madness, she said, moving to her husband's side, it would do his reputation no good at all. The doctor told her coldly to go and instruct the servants to prepare a room. It was soon after that, that Topher thought he'd solved the mystery – or part of it.

While there was movement below, he moved into his bedchamber, and through a crack in the floorboards – there was one by the side of his bed – he saw Kelley hand to the doctor a small glass bottle and an old book, which he said he'd found in the ruins of Glastonbury, the ancient seat of King Arthur. The bottle contained a red powder and the book – if only he could decipher its codes, he said – contained a recipe for the Philosopher's Stone!

Now Topher recalled another part of Kelley's reputation – as a scryer! This had come up during his trial, where he had denied it. But now he was boasting about it. *He* could read the crystals.

He could communicate with angels and if the two of them pooled their knowledge, he said, he was sure they would be able to satisfy the Queen.

But how did Kelley know of the Queen's command?

Why didn't his father ask this question?

Why, *why* did he believe that Kelley could do the things he claimed? He'd said that angels communicate best with innocent children, so why was he trusting a convicted criminal? Only one answer was possible – the doctor was desperate to fulfil the Queen's command. It was a question – for him – of life and death.

122

For days it seemed obvious – to everyone else – that the man was up to no good. He stayed, even though, on the very next day, the doctor was called away. He set off on horseback for Plymouth. Drake had been sighted approaching Plymouth after completing his circumnavigation of the world, the first Englishman to do it! Doctor Dee wanted to be the first to talk to him.

When he came back, fourteen days later – tired but in great good humour – Jane reported that Kelley had spent nearly all the time in the doctor's rooms reading his private papers. Doctor Dee assured her that Kelley had his permission to do so.

Topher was sure that Kelley's real reason for collaborating with Doctor Dee was not to help him, but to learn *his* secrets. Kelley thought Doctor Dee was close to discovering the secret of the Philosopher's Stone. That's why he'd come.

Kelley didn't do much scrying. As far as Topher could tell, whenever the doctor suggested it, Kelley said he was not in the right humour. Coming home from school one Thursday, Topher thought his father had realised Kelley's shortcomings, and gone back to his original plan, because he heard a girl's voice coming from the mirror room. Had he decided to use an innocent child after all?

'In seven thou shalt find the unity,' sang out a high, piping voice.

'In seven thou shalt find the trinity . . .'

On the pretext of looking for Ka who hadn't been at the door to greet him, Topher opened the door and crept in, but there was no little girl in the room. Ka was in the room – asleep on the floor below a chart of the

world with Drake's successful route marked upon it –
and so was Kelley who glared angrily at Topher, and
then at the doctor, who had a rapt faraway expression
on his face.

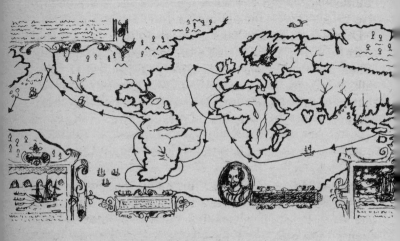

Kelley hissed, 'Leave, boy!'

But his father said, 'Let him stay. Let him hear the
maid.'

'What maid?' Topher still couldn't see anyone else in
the room.

Doctor Dee said, 'Madinia, our spirit guide, a
beautiful creature from the other side. Mr Kelley has
summoned her.' She was giving them useful information,
he said, that they must conjure with seven and not nine
as he had previously thought.

'Where is she?' Topher was suspicious.

The doctor said, 'In the crystal.'

This one was black, made of obsidian, his father said.

Looking into it, Topher couldn't see anything except green-black glass with bubbles in it. He certainly couldn't hear anything, but the doctor said if he waited he would hear wondrous things. But Kelley said he couldn't work with Topher in the room. He was a disruptive force. Topher picked up Ka.

Downstairs, he told Jane about the voice, and she said scornfully that it was Ned Kelley talking out of his belly. When he laughed she said, 'Really, Topher, it is belly-talk, stomach talk – *ventri loqui*.' Some people could do that, she said, speak out of their stomachs and make listeners think the voice was coming from somewhere else.

He said, 'Does my father know about this *ventri loqui*?'

She said he knew about it in theory, but still thought that Kelley had contacted a spirit from the other side. She was angry and upset that her clever husband had been so duped. A few days later, when she gave birth to a baby girl, Jane's joy at having a healthy baby and surviving the birth herself, was mixed with more anger, for Doctor Dee insisted on calling his daughter Madinia, after the spirit child!

Now the house in Mortlake was filled with new sounds, the cries of a baby, the rock of her cradle on the wooden floor and the rhythmic chant of the Seven Times Table. But the Seven Times Table worked no better than the Nine Times Table. It didn't bring forth the secret of the Philosopher's Stone nor of the wondrous Elixir.

Fortunately Doctor Dee was not devastated by this failure, but Kelley was angry. The doctor knew that

Drake's *Golden Hind* had returned laden with riches – rare spices, precious jewels and tons of silver. The Queen's coffers would soon be full and for the time being, at least, she didn't need the Philosopher's Stone.

Kelley's anger was directed at everyone in the house. No longer charming and silver-tongued, he went into great sulks in which he didn't speak to anyone for days. Topher didn't mind that, but he did mind when Kelley turned his anger on Ka, when he became obsessed with the idea that *she* was withholding the secret they were seeking. It was the Egyptian ankh on her forehead which gave him the idea, and the fact that she spent so long in the mirror room, looking at the crystals.

Chapter 19

It was a freezing cold day when it occurred to Kelley.
At least Topher thought afterwards that he'd witnessed
the moment. It was after Christmas and the low-beamed
living room was dark, though it was nearly midday.
Outside, the snow in the garden lay in thick hummocks,
making Topher, who was on the window seat with Ka,
think of the snow-beasts Frobisher had described. They
looked as if they might be sleeping there!

The doctor was away, summoned by the Queen to
cross the frozen Thames and hurry to Whitehall where
she was in residence. Jane sat by the fire rocking the
baby in its cradle, and Kelley was pacing the rush-strewn
floor.

'Be seated, Mr Kelley,' said Jane, though many a time
he had asked her to call him Ned. 'Be seated. You are
causing the ash to rise.'

But he didn't seem to hear her. She spoke softly for
fear of waking the baby, and he was thinking of other
things. Then he stopped suddenly and snapped his
fingers. The ash in the hearth rose in a cloud, the baby
started to wail and Topher realised he was staring at Ka,
and that she was staring at him. She looked quite angry.
Perhaps she could read his thoughts because suddenly
she sprang from the window seat and disappeared, a
second before Kelley stepped towards her. Even Topher

didn't see where she went.

Jane said, 'Don't worry, Topher,' as Kelley went in search of her, first to the kitchen, then back into the living room, then up the stairs, but Topher couldn't help worrying. When Kelley went upstairs he followed him and heard him moving around inside the mirror room.

'Puss. Pusskin!'

How stupid he was! Ka wouldn't come to him whatever he did.

A few minutes later he came out of the room – before Topher had time to disappear into his – holding a dead mouse which he must have got from a trap. Spinning it by the tail he smiled. 'Ah, Topher! When you see Ka, tell her I have a present for her.'

Then he went back into the mirror room.

When Topher went back to the living room Jane signalled that Ka was beneath her skirt.

Late that evening, as he lay in bed, with Ka safely beside him, Topher heard Kelley telling the doctor that he was sure the cat was their means to success – if they could but speak to her in her own language.

'What language is that?' the doctor asked in a tired voice lacking its usual lilt.

'Why, Egyptian of course,' Kelley replied.

'But it is a written language not a spoken one,' the doctor said. 'A picture language that few understand and no one can pronounce.'

'The cat knows it,' said Kelley stubbornly. 'The cat knows.'

'Do you?' Topher whispered to Ka, asleep on the feather mattress beside him.

Of cou . . . rrrse! Of cou . . . rrrse! she purred.

128

Why did the doctor keep Kelley on? Their work together seemed to be finished as far as the doctor was concerned. He had other things on his mind. The Queen was no longer pressing him to find the Philosopher's Stone – or the Elixir, for she seemed reconciled to her second cousin James Stuart succeeding her on the throne, if only it could be arranged. At present he was King of Scotland. If he became King of England it would unite the two countries and bring an end to wars between them. She hated wars – they were so expensive – yet a war with Spain looked increasingly likely. Francis Drake's success had enraged King Philip of Spain. He said that Francis had stolen the treasure he'd brought home to England – from Spanish ships, treasure intended for the king's coffers! The Queen had sent the king messages saying she was angry too, but she wasn't really. She wanted to reward Drake when he sailed the *Golden Hind* round to London. She wanted to knight him, make him Sir Francis Drake! But how could she do this without provoking war with Spain?

Doctor Dee was applying his brilliant mind to problems like these. He went to Scotland and he went to Spain.

In his absence, Kelley spent hours studying Ka, though she avoided him as much as she could. But Kelley followed all her movements, especially of her eyes. He seemed to think there was some mystical connection between the cat's pupils and the moon, for both waxed and waned, both could be round orbs or narrow slits. He made charts of both and tried to correlate the two. Topher saw them when he investigated, because he kept watch, of course; he did everything he could to keep Ka safe. It was obvious that Kelley thought that if he found the right time, the *auspicious* time, then Ka would speak, and tell him what he wanted to know.

Unfortunately Topher had to go to school every day but when he did Jane kept watch. She didn't like the way Kelley looked at the cat either. She didn't like the way he looked at anything – least of all her! And one day when Topher got home from school a triumphant Jane greeted him. She had turned Kelley away from the house. She had told him to pack his bags and go, for he had behaved unseemly towards her!

Topher was suspicious. Jane had told Kelley to go on other occasions and he'd taken no notice of her. And where was Ka? She hadn't appeared as she usually did when he arrived home. He went to the room where he'd noticed the charts of Ka's eye movements and the moon. The charts had gone. He called for Ka. She didn't come. It soon became obvious that she had gone.

First he ran to the landing stage, but none of the boatmen had seen Ka or Kelley. They promised to keep a lookout. Then he raced back to the house, stopping only to question whomever he met about whether they'd seen Kelley with or without a cat. Then, almost despairing because no one had seen them, he reached his own door again and noticed Mistress Pottle sitting in her window. Of course! If anyone had seen them go, it would be her. He knocked on her door and heard her call for Dickon, her serving man, but after what seemed an age, the latch lifted and her own furrowed face appeared in the doorway.

'Good day to you, Mistress Pottle.' It was no good rushing in, he had to remember his manners.

'Good day to you, Master Dee.'

'Have you seen Mister Kelley this day, Mistress Pottle?'

'I have,' she said slowly. Why wasn't Mistress Pottle a gossip? He needed information quickly.

'Have you seen my cat, Mistress Pottle?'

'I have, Master Dee.'

'Were they together, Mistress Pottle?'

'They were.'

He eventually learned that Kelley had left the house about three hours earlier with Ka in a wicker cage. They had left by the high road heading eastwards. It was now exactly six of the clock. He could hear St Mary's clock chiming. Kelley had had a three-hour start and all he knew was that he was heading east. He could be going almost anywhere, staying south of the river or crossing to the north further along the bank. Hoping that he'd find more informants along the way and that they'd be speedier than his neighbour, Topher set off. He must find Ka and he must find her quickly.

Chapter 20

Where was Kelley taking Ka? Where did he live, or where had he lived before he'd moved into the Dee household? As he strode along the mud road, the village of Mortlake soon behind him, Topher thought about these things, straining his brain to remember any gossip he'd heard. He'd said he'd come from Deptford, but that had been when he'd said he was Edward Talbot. Perhaps he should have consulted Jane? He should certainly have told her he was going – she'd be worried – but if he had told her she'd have forbidden him to go, and he had to go for Ka's sake.

With luck Kelley would have stopped at some tavern on the road ahead, might even be staying the night at one. With guile he might be able to rescue Ka – from Kelley's room perhaps while he supped beer below. Mistress Pottle said she'd been in a wicker cage, a bird cage like the one she kept her linnets in. Poor Ka – she'd hate that – but at least it made it easy to enquire about her.

'Have you seen a man with a cat in a cage?' There weren't many travellers about, but he asked them all, and he got his first lead at a cottage by the first cross roads. There was an old couple sitting outside in their garden, watching the evening sun go down.

'Have you seen a man with a cat in a cage?'

At first they didn't answer. Instead the old man questioned Topher. 'What be you doing, young gentleman, out on your own at nightfall?'

'I am on an errand for my master and I am in much haste.' He'd thought about questions he might be asked as he'd hurried through the countryside, glad that his clothes were of good quality. It wouldn't do to look like a common vagrant and be thrown in the stocks at the first village he came to.

'Who might that master be?' said the old man.

'Doctor Dee of Mortlake.'

The pair thought they had heard of him, even though he lived two mile hence. More importantly they had seen a man with a cat. He had taken the Southwark road they said. So Kelley was heading for London it seemed, avoiding the river where he knew Ka had many friends among the boatmen. If he was going to cross the Thames he would use London Bridge at Southwark.

Topher pressed on, even though it was nearly dark, accepting bread and ale from the old couple but declining their offer of a place on their floor for the night.

Fortunately it wasn't raining though it was April, the month of showers, and he didn't feel cold either though the air was fresh. The brisk pace he set kept him warm. Unfortunately, as it grew darker, his fears grew, fears for Ka, fears for himself. As the darkness thickened, harmless trees turned into witches and the echo of his own footsteps became thieves behind him. Only his greater fear – for Ka's safety – kept him putting one foot in front of the other, stopped him climbing a tree or crouching in a ditch.

Left right left right.

Left right left right.

Soon his feet felt sore.

Had he worn through the shoe leather?

Left right left right.

As he moved eastwards the cloud thinned and some stars appeared, then suddenly a full moon, and the frosty grass sparkled.

Left right left right.

How much further?

How far was Southwark?

A dog barked. A cock crowed, deceived by the moonlight into thinking it was morning. A barn owl screeched, then floated by him like a ghost.

Left. Right. Left. Right. He was slowing down and as he passed through a tiny village without a single light, sleep started to pull on his eyelids and drag on his feet. Then he saw the eyes of a cat in a hedge! It wasn't Ka but it made him think of her, and filled him for a while with energy. But he slowed again, couldn't help it as he passed through village after village and church bells tolled the hours away. Eight. Nine. Ten.

How many villages were there between Mortlake and Southwark? He lost count as he passed through them, but did at last see – dimly in the darkness – what he thought might be the buildings of a town. A church tower stuck out against the moonlit sky, and here and there a light flashed or flickered as if someone was carrying a flaming torch, or as if a door might be opening to reveal a roaring fire. As he got nearer he could hear and smell it – a mixture of sweat and dung and the river itself and the marshes which surrounded it. Laughter and raucous voices carried on the night air. Was no one sleeping? Was Kelley in one of those buildings ahead? Was Ka? Dogs barked. Something bellowed, so he must be near the bear gardens and the bull ring, and the theatres perhaps, for two more had sprung up on this side of the river, away from the City magistrates. He flattened himself against a wall as a woman rushed by him, hair streaming, then a man with his shirt hanging out. Fortunately they didn't notice him and he tried to recall his plan. What was it? Yes – to be as honest as he could, to say he was looking for Ned Kelley and, if pressed to say why, to say he had a message from Doctor Dee. But no, no . . . that was his second plan. His first was to walk round and see if he could see Kelley, because his chances of finding Ka would be better if Kelley didn't know he was there. But where should he begin? Now there were more people about and he was in a main street as far as he could see, which wasn't very far, but it was only one in a maze of streets which seethed with life. It wasn't a bit like any of the sleeping villages he'd passed through. From the light inside the buildings he could just make out the signs on the white walls outside – the Boar's Head, the Cardinal's Hat, the Gun, the Cross Keys, the Spurre, the Christopher, the Bear and Barge – he had never seen so many inns so close together, all with bodies pouring in or falling out of their doors. Weren't there any ordinary houses? Stepping over a body in an alley he tried to see through the horn

window of one of them and could just make out the shapes of men gathered round a table, heads close together, and possibly a woman standing by ready to fill their tankards from a jug, but there was no chance of recognising anyone, it wasn't possible to see their features.

'Oh! Isn't he a pretty one!'

Turning, he saw two brightly dressed ladies in the doorway of a house behind him and he was just about to ask if they knew Ned Kelley when they grabbed him. One in scarlet, slashed with grubby white said, 'He's mine!' but the other in yellow said they must share.

They wanted his hair, that was all, but it was horrible sitting on a stool while they cut it off, one either side of him, laughing a lot and calling him pretty creature and delicious boy. His hair wasn't so very long even before they started to cut it and they seemed to want every last inch. Blanche, the one in scarlet and the more talkative of the two, said that blond hair was the height of fashion. Frances, the other one, said they would get a wig made of it – like the Queen's. Topher thought of saying, the Queen's hair is red, but didn't say anything, just tried to keep still as his hair floated past him onto the women's slippered feet; the knives in their hands looked sharp. Blanche's breath stank of beer and cheese, but a pomade between her breasts threw out whiffs of musky perfume. He began to feel sleepy. It was after all the middle of the night and the room was warm – and more comfortable than some he'd glanced into. There were benches round the room with hassocks on them. What would the ladies do with him when they had finished? Turn him out into the dark night? What would he do then? He was thinking about this, when suddenly they declared they were finished. As Frances gathered up his hair, Blanche said he was a poor shorn lamb and put a cup of beer into his hand. Then, noticing how tired he was, she said he could stay, as long as he made himself scarce in the morning. Heavy with sleep, he felt himself being helped to lie down when the door opened and he heard a man's voice greeting the ladies cheerily, but despite thinking that the man's voice sounded familiar, he couldn't stop his eyes closing.

When he woke – to the sound of cartwheels on cobbles – it took him several minutes to remember where he was, though he could see Blanche and Frances sleeping, Frances, on a bench beneath a coverlet, her dress standing beside her like a headless woman, Blanche in a chair by the dead fire. She was still in the dress she'd been wearing last night, but she had taken off her farthingale which stood in the centre of the room like a large cage.

Cage! He remembered Ka!

Seeing the outlines of passers-by through the window, he realised he too ought to be on his way. Stiffly he stood up. He needed the jakes and he felt hungry. Picking up a crust of bread and hoping it wasn't stealing, he wondered what to do. He had no idea where Kelley was, that was the trouble. In the light of a new day, what he had done seemed very silly. Coming all this way was futile. How could he possibly find Kelley among all these people? There were scores of them just in the street outside. Wondering if he should wait and ask Blanche and Frances when they woke, or make himself scarce as they'd advised, he remembered the man who had arrived last night, remembered thinking that his voice had sounded familiar, just before he'd fallen asleep. Why, why had he thought it was familiar? Wishing he could think more clearly he examined the room again.

Then he saw it – in the pool of wax beneath a candlestick – a cat's paw print – or part of one – just two pad prints in fact and the marks of two claws – *as if a cat in a cage had been reaching out with a front paw – desperately.* Ka! He was sure of it! But surely she would have smelt him? Surely she would have miaowed? Perhaps she had, but he wouldn't have heard her. He *hadn't* heard her. Full of self hatred, but also a renewed sense of hope, he picked up the candlestick and put it down again with a bang, and as he hoped Blanche woke up.

In the morning light she reminded him of an old sow. Piggy eyes with pale lashes glared at him angrily.

'Who was that man?' He spoke before she did. 'Where was he going?'

Now she shrieked at Frances that the blackguard had gone without paying for his board.

'Where has he gone?'

It was some time before he got them to listen to him. Then they were pleased to be able to remember that he'd said he was heading for Deptford. Then they were miserable again saying he was probably heading for the docks and they'd never see him again. And he left while they were still lamenting Kelley's escape without paying, worried in case they wanted him to pay for his board, for he had but a penny in his pocket. Surely his hair was payment enough? Deptford, he knew, was eastwards, next to Greenwich. In the street he joined the steady stream of people coming from the direction of London Bridge, some on foot, some in laden carts. Passing a milestone which said that Greenwich was six miles away, he thought it might take him two hours on foot.

Fortunately he managed to get a lift – on a cart that was taking a load of grain to the storehouse by the Great Dock in Deptford itself. The carter whose name was Sam Browne was a fat cheerful man, with a row of pimples on his forehead that wobbled. They wobbled even more when he laughed which he did a lot. He was particularly cheerful about this assignment. The *Golden Hind* with Captain Drake aboard was on its way to Deptford he said, and Good Queen Bess was going to take delivery of the treasure he had won for her. Sam hoped to be there to see it, and others it seemed had the same idea.

As they left Southwark and entered rolling country-side the road east was busy. Topher kept a lookout for Kelley along the way, though he guessed he was several hours ahead. But, towards midday, as they reached the outskirts of Deptford, he thought he glimpsed a back he recognised on a cart ahead, and when he saw a birdcage wedged between some bales of fleeces he was even more sure. They were passing Sayes Court, the home of the lord of the manor according to Sam, a man called Sir Christopher Browne, who he was sure was a kinsman of his.

When he said, 'What think you of that, young Topher, me one of the gentry?' Topher couldn't think of anything to reply. His mind was full of other things, the main one being – how was he going to rescue Ka?

Chapter 21

Sam noticed him staring at the cart ahead and said, 'What's troubling you, Topher?'

'That man, I think he's got my cat.'

'If he's got your cat and it is your cat, you take your cat, young fellow.'

Topher explained the difficulty.

Fortunately the two carts seemed to be heading for the same place. Most of the traffic went straight on when they'd passed the towers and turrets of Sayes Court, but the wool cart turned left into a tree-lined road which led to the river and the storehouse. Now Topher climbed into the back of the grain cart. He was almost certain it was Kelley and didn't want him to turn and see him. Any doubts evaporated when Sam said, 'That man's hat, it sit unusually low on his head.'

When they reached the storehouse, a busy, noisy place near the docks, Kelley got down. Several river barges were delivering stuff too. There were a lot of people around, but Topher saw Ka when Kelley lifted the cage off the cart and set off eastwards at a brisk pace. Saying a hurried goodbye to Sam Topher followed, keeping hidden as much as he could. Kelley seemed to know where he was going. He walked purposefully – with no thought for Ka swinging from his hand – weaving in and out of people and pack animals, and carts, skirting a dry dock where men were working on a half-finished ketch. Beyond the dock was a row of artisans' workshops. Topher's fear was that Kelley would disappear inside one of them without his seeing him. He needn't have worried – for the moment anyway, for Kelley pressed on, striding along the Strand Road. Where was he heading? The village it seemed. They crossed the common and passed the church, and then Kelley turned sharp left joining a crowd of people heading for the river. There really were a lot of people, crowds of them, villagers and quite a lot of the travellers who had been on the road from London. The names of Drake and of Her Majesty were on all their lips. There was a spicy smell in the air. The *Golden Hind* was approaching, it seemed, with her cargo of cloves as well as silver. Everyone wanted to be at the dock to see her arrive.

As the crowd grew thicker it became harder to keep track of Kelley but – Topher took heart – it was easier too to keep hidden. He felt sure that Kelley hadn't seen him so far. But suddenly, as the river came into view, the crowd slowed down, stopped in fact as people started to line the riverbank and strain their necks to see downstream.

Kelley, though, pressed on, he seemed to be heading for some larger timber buildings just beyond. Poor Ka lurched to and fro. Topher longed to grab her and run, but he was more conspicuous now. As they came to the buildings – storehouses, he thought – he kept close to the wall. When Kelley stopped – at the door of one of them – so did he, further back. But when Kelley put Ka down for a moment, needing two hands to open the door, Topher took his chance. He ran forward and grabbed the cage.

And Kelley grabbed him, by the ear in a pincer grip. Then, opening the door and kick-closing it behind him, he hauled Topher inside a storehouse full of grain.

'You fell into that one, didn't you? Thought you were invisible, did you? Didn't you realise we needed you as well?'

What did he mean? Who were 'we'?

'The cat talks to you. I know that. Well, now you can make her talk to us.'

Kelley started to climb a staircase, still holding Topher by the ear. Reaching a landing he started to climb another one. Then reaching the top of that he kicked open a door and there, in a furnished room, sitting round a table, were three men Topher thought he recognised. Two looked like rough seafarers; one looked like a merchant. They'd been to the house in Mortlake, he thought, when Doctor Dee wasn't there. Kelley put the cage on the table and turned to Topher. 'Make the witch talk!'

'Ka isn't a witch!'

'Make her tell us the secret!'

'W-what secret?'

'The secret of the Stone, of course.'

'She doesn't know it. Nobody knows it.' What else could he say? But Ka's eyes were huge. She looked thin. He must do something to save her.

'She talks to you. I've heard her in your room at night. And she's got the devil's mark upon her,' said Kelley.

'That's a heathen cat if ever I saw one,' said one of the rough-looking men; he had three parallel scars across his cheek.

'A witch in cat form,' said one with a patched eye. 'It's obvious.'

'So make her talk,' said Kelley. 'In Egyptian.'

The merchant didn't say anything but he fingered a pistol on the table in front of him. Topher didn't know what to do. They were in a room at the front of the building facing the dock, but there was so much noise outside no one would hear him if he shouted. The crowd was cheering now. Perhaps they could see the *Golden Hind*. Certainly the smell of cloves was strong even in this room. The sun was shining. The day was warming up. Drake must be very near. He glanced out of the window.

'Don't think you can call on your famous friends,' said Kelley as Hawkins and Frobisher came into view, clearing a way for the Queen, who now appeared, followed by Walsingham and Sir Christopher Hatton and Doctor Dee!

'God Save Your Majesty! God Save Your Majesty!' roared the crowd, then a hush descended as she raised her hand.

'God bless you all, my good people.' Queen Elizabeth's voice rang out and the rings on her fingers sparkled in the sunlight.

'Make the cat talk or we will.' The man Topher called Patch was on his knees, his face pressed against the wicker cage. Ka hissed.

'How?' said Topher. 'How will you make her talk?'

'We'll go fishing with her,' said Patch and he sang softly:

'Green grow the rushes o!

We'll go dingle dangle
Till we know know know!'

He picked up the cage and held it at arm's-length, then mimed dropping it in the water. 'If she's a witch she'll float – and talk. If she's not she'll drown.'

The others laughed.

'Yes, we'll try her like any common witch,' said Three Scars.

A trial – the men warmed to that idea. They could do it right then, they said. If they took her out of the back of the building now, and did it further along the bank no one would notice. Topher tried to think clearly. Ka was in great danger. So was he. But they were so near help, if only he could contact it. Outside were some of the bravest and cleverest men in England and they were his friends. Shouting would be useless. The crowds were cheering again as if they were never going to stop. Glancing he saw the bowsprit of a ship coming into view, then the ship's figurehead, the golden hind itself, gleaming in the sunlight.

What else could he do? He needed time and he must get rid of these men.

He said, 'Ka does speak to me – sometimes – but only if we're alone.'

They were suspicious.

'He'll be out of that window before you can say Jack!' said Three Scars.

But Kelley was prepared to give him a chance. 'Two of us can stand below the window, and two outside the door. It wouldn't be in young Topher's interest to try and escape. He knows that.' He ran his finger along the blade of a knife and Patch volunteered to stand outside. The merchant stood up too, picking up his pistol. The silver inlay on its barrel flashed as it caught the sunlight. If only the sun keeps shining, thought Topher with sudden inspiration.

'I shall need a mirror,' he said to Kelley. 'You know that.'

Again Kelley agreed though the others didn't like the delay. They liked it even less when Kelley couldn't find a mirror. But then the merchant left the room and returned with a shiny silver plate. These rooms above the storehouse must be his living quarters.

Topher asked Kelley to prop up the plate so that he and Ka could see into it and while he did, Topher tried hard to remember some of the signals he'd seen his father make. Glancing out of the window to see where he could direct the beam of light which he hoped would lead to his rescue, he saw Patch leering up at him, unobserved by the crowd waiting for the gangplank of the *Golden Hind* to descend. There was no time to waste. Soon his father and Frobisher and Hawkins might be aboard the vessel. He moved to open the door of the cage, but Kelley objected.

Topher said Ka wouldn't speak unless she was free – and not if anyone else was present.

Reluctantly Kelley left the room.

Then Topher opened the cage and Ka stepped out. She was very calm. He stroked her and she acknowledged his affection with a soft chirruping sound, but didn't demand more. She knew as well as he did that they must get on. This was a test for both of them.

'O Ka!' said Topher in a clear voice that he hoped

Kelley could hear. 'O Ka! Cat of many lives! O Ka! Tell to me, the secret of eternity!' As he spoke he lifted the silver plate and carried it towards the window. Then he tilted it so that it caught the sun's rays.

There was a knocking on the door. Kelley was impatient.

'O Ka! Everlasting cat!

O Ka! Tell to me . . .'

He tilted then straightened the plate.

'The secret of eternity!'

He tilted then straightened the plate again so that the light bounced off the Queen's jewelled hand.

'Say something, Ka. Say anything,' he whispered.

The door handle rattled and Ka began to wail. She went on and on as if she might really be speaking, 'Mwa! Mwa! Mwa! Mwaaaa! Mwaaaa! Mwaaaa!'

And Topher played the beam of light on the Queen's hand.

'What's she saying?' The door handle rattled again, Ka went on wailing and Topher went on bouncing the light off the ring on the Queen's finger.

Flash flash flash. Flaaaaa . . . sh! Flaaaaa . . . sh! Flaaaa . . . sh!

'What's she saying?' Kelley was impatient.

'Mwa! Mwa! Mwa!'

Flash flash flash.

As Ka wailed Topher rocked the silver plate up and down, up and down, till it grew heavy in his hands. When would someone notice? His father was standing right by the Queen but all eyes were now focused on the gang-plank of the *Golden Hind*. The crowd was silent now, waiting for Drake to appear.

'Mwaaaa!'

His father noticed! Looked up. Looked back at the Queen's ring for several seconds. Looked up again to the window of the merchant's house. Unfortunately he couldn't see Topher who was standing back because he didn't want Patch to see what he was doing, but he hoped he had signalled – Save Us. Perhaps he had because he saw his father nudge Hawkins.

But then the door opened and Kelley burst into the room, Three Scars just behind him.

Fortunately Ka responded by intensifying her wail. She threw back her head and gave forth sentence after sentence of it. It transfixed the men.

'What's she saying?'

'That ... er ... there are several planes of existence,' said Topher playing desperately for time. 'That ... er ... we die to live again.'

'How?' said Kelley. 'Tell us how!'

Topher heard something outside beneath the window – a scuffle and a thud. He heard a bang which might have been a pistol, then the sound of footsteps running up the stairs. Then, Kelley grabbed him as the door crashed open – and there was the bulk of Hawkins and of Frobisher blocking anyone's escape.

But Kelley held Topher in front of him.

'Harm me and the boy gets it!' said Kelley, his knife against Topher's throat, as Ka came flying at Kelley's face. With a cry he dropped the knife. Then Hawkins grabbed him as someone burst through the window.

Then from outside there was a terrible groaning sound which stopped everyone for a moment. But suddenly it was action again as fists flew and bodies fell to the floor.

Hearing a cry of 'Run!' Topher ran down the stairs, hesitating only to see that Ka was with him. In fact she was soon ahead of him, racing out of the door and onto the dock where chaos reigned because there had been a terrible accident. They soon learned that the groaning sound had been the dockyard bridge giving way, tipping hundreds of people into the water.

Then Doctor Dee was by his side, pointing to Drake who was kneeling on the deck of the *Golden Hind* at the feet of Queen Elizabeth. The doctor said that the Queen said she wouldn't begin the dubbing ceremony till she knew that all her good people were safe – and that included Topher. A sailor was about to pull up the gangplank to stop other loyal citizens clambering aboard, when the Queen held up a restraining hand.

'It is Ka and Topher and Doctor Dee. They will have luncheon with us.'

Then Topher and Ka went aboard the *Golden Hind*.

Chapter 22

Francis Drake welcomed Ka, saying he was honoured to
have her aboard. Then he greeted Topher warmly, first
hugging him, then holding him at arm's-length to see
how much he'd grown in his three-year absence. Topher
couldn't help staring at the white scars on Francis's suntanned face, just beneath his eye. They were nothing,
Francis said, arrow wounds, that was all. He'd been
peacefully watching some birds called ostriches – strange
birds who stuck their heads in the sand and couldn't fly
– when Indians on the Island of Mocha had fired at him.

Queen Elizabeth laughed. 'Maybe those birds were
trying to tell you something, Francis!'

Inside the wainscotted main-cabin, furnished with
cushions and tapestries like a rich man's house – for
Francis loved luxury even when he was sailing – the
table was laid with plates and spoons and dishes and
tankards, made of richly patterned gold!

'Aztec gold, captured from the godless Spanish,'
Francis said, lifting a goblet and handing it to the Queen,
who called him a wicked pirate, but she laughed as she
said it.

However, during the meal – of roast swan stuffed
with quail stuffed with partridge, followed by apple cake
flavoured with cinnamon, followed by syllabub made
with thick Devonshire cream – she told Francis that she

151

could not personally knight him herself, as that would offend the Spanish who might wage war on England, so the French ambassador would perform the ceremony.

Everyone went quiet then, except the musicians, Francis's own musicians who had sailed all round the world with him because he liked to listen to music while he ate. They carried on playing their viols, but not so well, and the Queen looked angry. But then word arrived that the people who had fallen off the bridge, two hundred

152

subjects coming to see her, had all been rescued – not a single one had drowned – and the Queen clapped her hands with joy and everyone inside clapped too, and the crowd outside began to shout, 'God Save Your Majesty!' as Hawkins and Frobisher appeared. Coming aboard, they said that Kelley and company had been clapped in irons to await trial.

A few minutes later, led by Her Majesty, they all went

ashore. First the Bishop gave thanks to God for their great good fortune, then in a breathless hush, Francis Drake knelt at the feet of the Queen who handed a sword to the French ambassador. But *she* said, 'Arise, *Sir* Francis Drake!' as the ambassador laid the sword on his shoulder, and Sir Francis Drake arose to tumultuous cheers.

Ka watched all this from the forecastle of the *Golden Hind*, and late that afternoon Topher climbed up to sit with her as they sailed up the Thames towards the City of London. The sun was setting over the Abbey of West Minster, and as they came in line with the Tower of London and cannon roared in thunderous salute, the ravens of the Tower rose in a cloud, glossy black against the red-gold sky, before wheeling and swirling high above the fluttering flags. Then, as the *Golden Hind* began to turn in towards Lyone's Key, Topher noticed one of the birds break free of the others and start to fly towards the ship. Ka noticed it too. It was doing acrobatics over the water, swooping low then soaring high, its finger-tip wings slanting first one way then the other.

But on the main-deck below no one seemed to notice it. All eyes were on Sir Francis, steering the vessel into the quay, while skilfully avoiding the smaller craft that had come out in scores to greet him, and as the wind ruffled his curly hair and lifted his short cape, the raven landed beside Topher on the forecastle.

The bird looked huge, compared with Topher and Ka! What was happening? Had he drunk too much Devonshire cider at luncheon? Round yellow eyes stared at them both. Then Ka, who *was* smaller, sprang onto its back and now the bird's ramp-like tail was beside Topher who stepped onto it, clambered up and took his place behind the cat. Far below, the waters of the Thames streamed towards the sea. Then as the bird with a massive surge of energy soared into the air, the silver Thames was even further below, was a sparkling ribbon on a robe of green, then a sparkling thread on that green robe as the bird flew higher and higher and faster and faster and faster still till, as Topher and Ka slept on its back, it travelled faster than the speed of light breaking barriers of space and sound and time.

* * *

Then it landed in Lyntone Road.

'Topher, come in. What are you doing out there in your pyjamas?'

He looked up and there was Molly at the window, except that there wasn't a window, no windowpanes anyway and there was a burnt-out car outside the house. He remembered what had happened and froze.

Then Molly came out of the house. But what about his dad? He daren't ask and began to shake as Molly put her arm around him – and he liked her arm around him.

'Don't worry about your dad,' she said. 'He's going to be all right, though they've kept him at Addenbrooke's overnight.'

His dad was in hospital with cuts and burns. So was a young man called Ewan who had been under the car when it exploded. He was very seriously injured.

'And Ka's come back,' she said. 'Look.'

She was on the doorstep.

'You'd think she'd been away for years not days,' Molly said when they were inside. 'Look at the way she's eating that Whiskas.'

Next day they went to see his dad – Molly's hero. He had saved her life she said – for Chris Hope had insisted on looking underneath the car before Molly even approached it. He had actually seen the young man attaching the bomb to the underside of the car, and was turning towards the house to ring 999 when the bomb had exploded before the young man had time to get out.

In hospital they got a glimpse of him too. Watched by police, he was in intensive care but was refusing to take any treatment which had been tested on animals. At school later, Petra said he was a hero, risking his life for the cause.

But he'd risked Molly's life too and his dad's – more than risked them – he'd *intended* Molly to die and didn't care if his dad or anyone else had got killed too. What sort of hero was that?

At half-term he and Ka went to stay with Ellie and the Wentworths and that was one of the things they talked about. On the Tuesday they went to the National Maritime Museum, where Topher hoped he might be able to tell Ellie about his time-travelling. There was a special exhibition on – about Francis Drake. He hoped it would help show Ellie what Francis was like, and what it was like living in the sixteenth century, but it was horribly disappointing. He should never have gone inside, should have been warned by the poster outside. It was at the top of the steps leading to the grand pillared entrance.

Sir Francis Drake
(1542–1596)
Ice! Water! Fire!
Master Mariner or Master Thief?

Master thief? That was what his enemies called him, the Spanish who wanted to invade England! If they had they'd have burned and tortured people, just as Bloody Mary had when she was married to King Philip of Spain. They had to be stopped and Francis had stopped them!

And yet, almost as soon as they got in the darkened room which held the exhibition, Ellie said, 'He was a master murderer as well, if you ask me. I hope he's not a hero of yours, Topher.' She was looking at a painting of a burning town. 'Did you know he burned Santiago to the ground, just because he couldn't find any treasure there?'

'*And* he executed one of his own men,' said Russell pointing to another picture.

'*And* he was a slave trader,' said Luke.

Mrs Wentworth said, 'It isn't Topher's fault! Leave him alone.'

But he felt as if it was his fault, that was the trouble. He certainly felt as if he ought, no wanted, to be sticking up for Francis – because Francis Drake had been his *friend*, that was why! A friend he'd wanted to tell Ellie about, even boast about, but how could he do that now? There was nothing here that gave any idea of what Francis was like. There wasn't even a decent picture of

157

the *Golden Hind*, not one that showed how colourful she was, nor that showed the ship's figurehead, the golden hind itself, that had gleamed so brightly in the sunshine. And all that remained of the little ship – that Queen Elizabeth said must be preserved for ever – was a chair. A *chair!* It was made, so a caption said, of the only bit of timber remaining from the *Golden Hind* which had been kept for a hundred years and then allowed to rot. That chair said as much about the *Golden Hind* as this exhibition did about Francis and Topher wanted to go home.

'What's the matter?'

When he didn't reply Ellie wandered off, and just for a moment, in his mind's eye, he saw Francis Drake stroking Ka as he welcomed her aboard his *colourful* ship. He saw his suntanned hand on the shiny red and yellow stripes of the handrail. He saw the red and golden lions of England and the blue and gold fleur-de-lys of France on her freshly painted sides, and the red on white crosses of the Saint George flag flapping in the breeze, and he *felt* the hand of Sir Francis Drake touching his as he handed him, Topher Hope, a blood red orange from Spain.

When they got back to the Wentworths' Ka was waiting and his dad and Molly arrived by car soon afterwards and Mrs Wentworth rang for pizzas. While they waited for them to be delivered they talked about the exhibition and had one of those long discussions the Wentworths specialised in – about religion and politics and morality and whether human nature had changed over the years.

'Who are our heroes now?' asked Mrs Wentworth,

waving a slice of pizza.

The talk went on and on.

'Who are our villains?' said Mr Wentworth.

Topher didn't say anything. He just sat with Ka who seemed to know that he needed her close, for only she understood. Only she had been there with him. It was impossible to explain, but he was sure that Francis had been a good man *in his time.*

On the way back to Cambridge Molly said suddenly, ' "The past is a foreign country. They do things differently there." That's what Hartley said.'

And that seemed sensible – like Molly – for that's what it felt like now, as if he'd been to a foreign country.

'What do you think, Ka?' She purred as she slept beside him on the back seat, seemed pleased to be back in the twentieth century. He lifted her onto his lap.

What a cat! What a survivor – and so was he!